AMBUSCADE
by
Orlando Rigoni

Author of "The Pikabo Stage" *and*
"Six-Gun Song"

Sabado, meaning Saturday in Spanish, was aptly named. For six days a week it sat and burned in the desert sun, its shingles warped, its paint scabbed, waiting for Saturday night when the boys came in from the ranches. Often it was a night of killing and thieving, with the sanctuary of the border only a few miles to the south.

Tony Egan know the town well, knew its blisters of vice, its alleys of sudden death, its vendors of rotgut and sedition. But it had been five years since the last time he had seen it, five long years behind bars.

Now he was waiting for two people: the man who had killed Tony's best friend, put a bullet in Tony, smashed his face to a pulp, and framed him for the killing; and the woman whose memory had sustained him during the months behind bars.

AMBUSCADE

AMBUSCADE

by

ORLANDO RIGONI

PRESTIGE BOOKS
NEW YORK, NEW YORK

Prestige Books, Inc.
18 East 41st Street, New York, New York 10017

Printed in the United States of America

CHAPTER ONE

Tony Egan, his slouch hat pulled low over his eyes to shade them from the hot, unfamiliar sun, rode his crow-bait horse down the slant toward the cluster of brooding shacks named Sabado. Sabado meant Saturday in Spanish, and that was what it was, a Saturday town. It sat and burned in the desert sun, its shingles warped, its paint scabbed, for six days a week, waiting for Saturday. Saturday night was the night the boys came in from the ranches—the cowboys, the vaqueros, and sometimes the foremen and the major-domos. Often it meant a night of killing and thieving, with the sanctuary of the border just a few miles south. It was a purgatory where men stopped to expel their venom on their way to hell.

Egan's lean, sallow face was a grim mask as he studied the town with brown eyes that glared like agate under heavy brows. He knew the town well, knew its blisters of vice, its alleys of sudden death, its vendors of rotgut and sedition. It was an oasis where a man could dis-

gorge his pent-up hate of merciless sun, choking sand
and ornery cattle. The price was no object and the hangover something to be endured, just so for one night they
could talk with other men, spend their money freely and
feel a woman in their arms.

Egan ran a lean hand over his face, feeling the
bristles. Five years of confinement can bleach a man's
skin; five years of prison fare can gaunt a man's bones.
He fingered the bullet on his watch chain. The watch had
been his father's; the warden had given it back to him.
The gun on his hip had been his father's, too. But the
bullet on his watch chain was his; it had been given to
him by Carl Dirkes, and he had carried it with him until
he had crawled half-dead from his saddle in Nacozapas,
across the border.

A fat woman at the cantina had dug the bullet from
him, but she could do nothing for his face; his face
that had been trampled and smashed by Carl Dirkes'
boots. It hadn't been much of a face, with its smashed
nose, its swollen eyes and torn cheeks. Even his jaw
was unhinged, and his talk was a garble of sound. His
mistake had been in not killing Dirkes when he had the
chance, for which he had Wilma Logan to thank—Wilma,
who had solemnly told him that she loved him. Instead,
he had watched Dirkes kill Patch Roger, his best friend.
He had downed Dirkes and fled, but Dirkes hadn't
stayed down. When he had come to, Dirkes had blamed
the killing of Patch on him and had shouted murder

to the law. Using his power and influence, Dirkes had had him extradited from Mexico and tried in a court that didn't know the meaning of justice.

He had been lucky to get off on a charge of manslaughter with a sentence of five years that had seemed like a hundred. Yes, he knew the town and the people in it; even the good people. Now he was coming back to balance an account that was long overdue.

He passed the town dump on the outskirts of Sabado and noticed that it had increased in size and stink. A mangy dog was rooting in the filth and garbage.

He passed Boot Hill and gave it a long, hard look. Patch must be up there, buried in a box. Somebody must have had the heart to do that for him. Egan again ran a hand over his face, feeling the unnatural smoothness of the skin where whiskers failed to grow. The young doctor at the prison hospital had done a good job of rebuilding his face, except that he had lost the blueprint of his features. He had taken skin from the smooth places on his body and had grafted them to his face. It was a new kind of surgery, the doc had explained, and Egan, with nothing to lose, had let the doctor experiment as he wished.

The doctor had given him a face—a great improvement over the mutilated thing he had brought to prison with him—but it was not his face. It was the face of a man who had never lived, without sun wrinkles, worry lines, or even the scars and moles the flesh is heir to.

It was a new slate waiting to be chalked and scribbled on. It was a mask to hide the worms of hate and the lust for revenge that lived under it. Nobody in Sabado would recognize him, and that suited him fine. He needed a name to go with the face. Brad Regan would do.

He reached the main drag of the town and rode his crow-bait at a steady pace along the ribbon of dust that was flanked with gaudy false fronts. The buildings at that end of town were daubed like Jezebels with paint to catch the eye. The Red Garter bar was still there, and the Sabado Queen. There was a pile of ashes where the Bull's-Eye had stood. It was miraculous that none of the other deadfalls had burned with it. The Chuckwagon Café was sporting a banner of smoke from the kitchen range, and the barbershop was doing business as usual. The few men who braved the hot sun on the creaky boardwalk, paid him little heed, even though he was an odd character in his bib overalls and the tacky gear the warden had given him. He still had most of the ten dollars going-away money from the prison's separation fund donated by a "generous" government.

An open space divided the two sections of town, a quarantine area separating the good from the bad. Beyond the open space was the general store, the doctor's office, lawyer Hicks' office, the post office and several other businesses, including a dressmaker. Next to the dressmaker's was Lupe's Café. Egan dismounted in front of the post office and dallied his horse to the rail. He mounted the plank walk, his cheap boots thudding upon the loose boards. He walked deliberately like a pilgrim getting his first view of the town. As he neared Andy Hicks' office, he slowed his pace and, reaching the door, opened it and looked in. Hicks had been the prosecutor at the trial, and now he sat behind his desk, as smug and well-fed as a gopher in a cornfield.

Hicks looked up, frowning. "What can I do for you, mister?"

Hicks' tone implied yokels had little business in his office.

"I was just wondering if you could give me the correct time, sir," Egan replied.

"You've got a fancy watch chain on your chest. Isn't there a watch to go with it?"

"It hasn't been running true lately," Egan said.

Impatiently Hicks pulled out his heavy gold watch. "It's twelve thirty-five."

"Thank you, sir," Egan said, backing out of the door.

Hicks hadn't recognized him; that was good. His quarrel with Hicks was secondary. Hicks had been forced to prosecute him, and he had tried to get him hanged, but the judge had seen through the fabricated evidence and had insisted on the manslaughter charge. Tony Egan walked on, and as he passed the dressmaker's shop he paused, surprised. He had not expected to see Ruby Miller still running the shop, yet there she was putting some hats in the display window. She looked right at him through the polished window glass, and their eyes met. She was the same beautiful woman, with her wavy copper hair, her frank brown eyes and her mobile mouth. Her straight nose gave her a queenly appearance.

Tony smiled at her and felt the smooth skin of his face pull with the effort. Ruby smiled back, and he doffed his hat, exposing bleached hair that was combed straight across his forehead to end in long sideburns on either side. The sideburns had a purpose; they concealed the scars where the skin had been tucked and sutured. He replaced his hat and moved on.

Egan turned into Lupe's Café, filled with noonday eaters. He was surprised at the number of diners, since the streets were so deserted. Like all desert animals, men seek shelter from the noonday sun. He found a place at the scrubbed counter, and Lupe came to take his order, as prim and crisp as ever. She had long black hair which she braided and coiled about her head like a crown. Her dark eyes were as mischievous as ever, too, and she had a voice as spicy as some of her Mexican dishes.

"What's for you, *amigo?*"

There was no recognition in her brown eyes, and Tony felt his masquerade must be complete.

"I'll have your regular comida, *señorita.*"

Her brown eyes frowned. "You from across the border, *señor?*"

"Sometimes." Tony smiled through his whiskers.

"We get many such. *Como se llama usted?*"

"My name? I'm called Brad Regan."

"I am Lupe. You look hungry, sodbuster. The *comida* today is bistek, frijoles, tortillas, and apple pie."

"*Bueno,*" Egan said. "But I'm no sodbuster."

Lupe shrugged. "You look like sodbuster. You too young to be *bandido.*"

"Appearances can be deceiving, Lupe." He used her name deliberately. "I'm no *bandido.*"

"Your skin too white. You been sick?"

"If I ever get some food, it might rosy my cheeks up some."

"Hokay. I bring the *comida.* No *cafe* for you; for you, *leche.*"

"But I don't like milk."

Lupe put her hands on her ample hips. "You going to eat here, you going to look more better. I don't want no customer looking pale like you; it is too much bad for business. You drink *leche.*"

She strutted out with a defiant toss of her head. A man near Tony let out a chuckle. He was a man with a double chin and an amplified stomach.

"If you want to stay thin, eat at Chinaman Charley's. Lupe will fatten you up if she loses money on the deal. Look at me. They used to call me ramrod, and they didn't mean ranch foreman, neither."

Tony recognized the man as one who used to side Carl Dirkes, but he had not been there the day of the beatings. His name was Bud Wilson.

"Reckon I could stand a little suet on my bones," Egan said.

"What are you?" The man looked Tony up and down, taking in his slouch hat, his bib overalls and his cheap boots. "You aimin' to homestead hereabouts?"

"Maybe," Tony said laconically.

"Don't. First off, you'd starve to death; second off, Carl Dirkes won't like it; and third off, I can offer you a job as flunky for the cook on my spread."

"I don't like a man telling me what I can and what I can't do."

"You don't know Carl Dirkes. Rub him right and you'll get along here. You'd better take the kitchen job I offered until you put some beef on your bones."

Rub Carl Dirkes the right way? He meant to do just that; he meant to rub him completely out. But Wilson had a point: he could do with some building up.

"Thanks, Wilson. I'll think about the job and let you know later."

"Later I'll be down in Honkytown, on the other side of the clearing. There's a rough crowd there Saturday nights. They don't take kindly to sodbusters."

"I'll let you know," Tony repeated as Wilson got up to leave.

Lupe brought his food, and he applied himself to it,

thinking of all the scurvy prison chow he had eaten in the last five years. He wanted to draw Lupe into conversation, but she was too busy to talk to him. He ate his apple pie—with milk—and found another wedge appear miraculously on his plate. He ate that, too, and he gulped the milk that came with it. He tried to pay for the extra pie and milk, but Lupe wouldn't even take the price of the meal.

"You pay me by the week, savvy? You pay now maybe you no come back. Buy yourself some pants and *chaparajos*. Not wear this beebee thing here." She pulled the suspenders of his overalls.

He decided to humor her. "*Muchas gracias*, Lupe. You now have a customer for life."

He went out into the sunlight and watched a lizard skitter under the boardwalk. He looked up at the church and thought about Wilma. Perhaps she wasn't even in town any more, much less still playing the organ at church. On an impulse he walked up the street a few steps and turned into Ruby Miller's store.

He blinked his eyes to accustom them to the shady interior, and stared at the bolts of cloth and ribbons on the counter. Behind the counter, her earrings twink'ing like tiny stars, stood Ruby. She had an enigmatic smile on her red lips and an amused question in her brown eyes.

"Hello," she said. "What can I do for you?"

Tony answered with a slow smile of his own. "I reckon

it's no frock or bonnet I want, ma'am. I want some infomation."

"That's the cheapest thing I sell," she answered in her low voice.

"And sometimes a most bounteous gift. There used to be a girl in this town named Wilma Logan. Is she still here?"

The smile on Ruby's lips flattened out, and a shuttered look glazed her eyes.

"Who are you to be asking?" she said flatly.

Egan was taken aback by the change in her expression and the tone of her voice.

"I'm Brad Regan," he said evenly. "I met a cousin of hers in Tucson. He asked me to look her up."

Ruby brushed back her red hair and inspected him from boots to slouchy hat. He felt uncomfortable under her frank appraisal and took his hat off.

"You look like a dirt farmer to me. I doubt Wilma would be interested in your kind," she finally said.

Tony felt rebuked by her answer, and his face hardened. The skin of his face might be new and unblemished, but the man beneath it was the same man with five years of bitterness thrown in.

"Don't you reckon Wilma can decide that for herself?"

"Perhaps. I'm just trying to save you from humiliation."

Tony ran a tongue across the whiskers on his lips.

"You talk as though Wilma were a Jezebel. Her cousin described her as a kindly girl who played the organ at church and was helpful to those in need."

"Her cousin has evidently not seen her for a long time. People change; they bend with the winds of fortune, or they break. Take my advice and forget Wilma Logan, as you call her. There are other women in Sabado more easily met and more receptive."

"You mean in Honkytown, Miss Miller—or is it Mrs. Miller?"

He could see her jaw harden. "It's Miss Miller, and I'm not easily met. At least some of the girls in Honkytown are honest. You get what you pay for."

Tony did not like the way the conversation was going. "Will you answer me one thing?" he inquired.

"What is it?"

"Is she still in town?"

"She's still around. She has changed. Her cousin wouldn't know her."

"How would I know her should we meet?" Tony asked blandly.

"When you see the best kept woman in town, that will be her," Ruby said with a touch of bitterness in her voice. Then she leaned forward and added, "Haven't I seen you somewhere before?"

Tony stiffened. Too much inquisitiveness might give him away.

"Reckon not, ma'am. Thanks for the information."

"I gave you none."

He turned on his heel and put his hat on his reddish hair. He said as he went out the door, "Us redheads ought to stick together."

As he walked toward his horse, he mulled over what Ruby Miller had told him and he didn't like the thoughts she had generated in his mind. He wondered about the sudden rash of organs; was that part of being kept? He shrugged the thought off.

"Why don't you practice on the new organ?" Tony asked feeling there was lack of generosity involved.

"I can't, mister. It takes a boy in the back to push the stick up and down."

"I won't keep you from your practicing, you're doing real well," Tony said as he turned to go.

He mounted and headed back toward Honkytown. Finding the livery barn, he put up his horse. The afternoon was wearing on, and already men were drifting in from the ranches.

"What's the livliest place in town now that the Bull's-Eye has burned down?" Tony asked the stable man.

"Was you here when the Bull's Eye was goin'? That was a humdinger of a place, an' pure honest."

"How come it was the only place that burned?" Tony asked.

"Some say," the stable man lowered his voice, "that Carl Dirkes had the fire set. He couldn't buy the place because Hackett wouldn't sell. Burning it was cheaper, and it cut down the competition. Now Dirkes has things his own way, him and that fancy new wife of his.

"New wife? What became of his old wife?"

"She was killed in 'a runaway. She always drove fractious hosses. Somebody spooked them one night, and when they found her her neck was broke."

"It must've been a hard blow for Dirkes," Tony hazarded.

"I dunno. He took it like he takes everything. He's iron-hard an' plumb quiet. They didn't get along a-tall. She roweled him like she roweled them wild hosses of hers. If you ask me, he could have been the one who spooked her team. He's a changed man since he got his new missus; he's got more pride, an' he's doin' things for the town on the other side of the clearing."

"You haven't answered my first question," Tony said.

"You asked about the liveliest place in town. Wal, let me see. The Red Garter has the hottest action, but I don't reckon a sodbuster like you would last long there. The Sabado Queen has taken on some class since Dirkes' second marriage. His wife sings there."

The last statement startled Egan. He had no further time to delve into Dirkes' activity if he expected to get a shave. The barbershop would be swamped later on.

"Thanks," Tony said. "Feed that crow-bait of mine real good; I might want to trade him off later on."

At the barbershop he was second in line, and while he waited his turn he read the weekly newspaper. As he scanned the news, one thing became apparent. Carl Dirkes, the man he had come back to kill, and his new wife hogged most of the news. Dirkes was adding the Lazy W to his holdings, having bought the spread from Waller's widow to help her get back to relatives in the East. Egan scoffed at the idea that Dirkes had done anything for charity. He had probably been the cause of Waller's death and had cheated the widow out of half the ranch.

Another item: Dirkes had redecorated the Sabado Queen. Still more: Dirkes was donating land for a schoolhouse. Mrs. Dirkes got her share of notices. She was planning an affair to raise money for the poor and orphaned children; she was adopting another little girl to join the boy she had already adopted. There was another item in larger type on the front page about the holdup of the Las Cruces stage, in which the passengers had not been molested but a shipment of gold from the Tucson area had been stolen. Tony felt the item had not received the prominence it deserved.

His turn came to take the chair, so he put the paper down and submitted to the sheet which the barber put around him.

"Shave," he said laconically.

The barber reached for the mug of lather but hesitated before daubing Egans' face.

Mister, you got the smoothest, whitest skin I ever seen on a man. You sure you ain't no girl wearing pants?"

"You'll have to take my word for that," Tony said. "I've got some whiskers."

"There ain't but two places I know a man can get so pallid; one is in the mines and the other—"

Tony cut him off, knowing what he was going to say. "I've been working in a hardrock mine up north. The damp and dark can bleach a man right down to his bones."

The barber daubed and stropped and scraped in silence. When he was heating the wet towel for the second time, Egan talked.

"This man Carl Dirkes and his wife cast a long shadow hereabouts," he said.

"You better believe it, pilgrim. He used to be one *malo hombre*. His first wife was some fancy she-cat."

He didn't have to tell Tony about Dirkes' first wife, Felicitas. She had made sure that everybody knew her and respected her.

"I hear he's a changed man," Tony said just before the scalding towel muffled his tender face.

"It's unhealthy to think otherwise, and that's a fact," the barber said, and clammed up.

When Tony climbed out of the chair, he rubbed his stinging face and looked at himself in the cracked mirror. He was surprised at how young he looked, with his uncreased face and his hollow cheeks. His brown eyes looked out from under the bony ridges of his brows, strangely at odds with the smooth white face they inhabited. His eyes were old, bitter, with the tiger of revenge stalking in their depths. As Wilson had said in Lupe's Café, he had better take that kitchen flunky job until his bones filled out.

He walked the length of the street, found a vantage spot where he wouldn't be noticed and studied the lay of the land as riders came shooting into town, overflowing with exuberance. He saw one group coming in, blasting the twilight with their upraised guns.

Egan stiffened in the shadow of the store front. He recognized Dirkes' foreman, Blackie Folger and his segundo, Vern Veldon. Folger had been there at the beating when Patch Roger had been killed. Veldon had been there, too, but Veldon was too sly to commit open murder; he had other ways. Carl Dirkes might have reformed, but he kept the same fast-gun, hard-fist crew on his payroll. Grim-lipped, Tony watched them disappear into the Red Garter. He gave them time to get settled and savor their first round of drinks. It was almost dark when he moved from his sentry post and legged it toward the batwing doors of the gaudy red building.

CHAPTER TWO

Tony slipped in through the batwing doors and scooted to one side, his back against the wall. The hanging lamps had been lit and the row of bracket lamps behind the bar cast a mellow golden light on the bottles and glasses stacked there. The lamplight mercifully softened the stained and blemished walls and turned the sawdust on the plank floor into a tawny carpet. The card tables were puddles of green at one side of the room. The lamplight could do nothing for the acrid cigarette smoke and the smell of sour whiskey that pervaded the place.

Already voices were raised in raucous camaraderie as Tony studied the backs of the men at the bar. His skin crawled as he thought of what might happen if Folger and Veldon knew who he really was. As he watched, the voices at the bar took form. The cowboys in their warped chaps, their high heels jingling with spurs, and their tall Texas hats looked like caricatures lined up at the bar, or puppets operated by invisible strings. They were giving somebody the roust, teasing and hurrahing some hapless victim they had chosen as the butt of their jokes. It wasn't until the man in the middle of the line turned his head and looked warily around the crowded room that Tony Egan discovered the man was a Negro.

"Come on, Abe Jones; let's see you finish a bottle in one breath!" one of the men jibed.

Abe Jones said in a sonorous voice, "You'all funnin' me 'cause I'se black. Why foh you want to make me drunk?"

"We ain't never seen a drunken black man before," Folger guffawed. "I'll pay for the bottle."

Abe looked around again like an animal seeking cover, and Tony saw the look of pleading in his dark eyes.

"All I want is to have mah fun jest like the rest of you."

"Come on, Abe; bottoms up!" somebody yelled, to the amusement of the others.

"It ain't fitten foh a man to slop his guts with p'izen in one gulp an' then grovel on the flooh lak' a dog. I'm a black man, I knows that, but I got mah pride jest lak' the rest of you gen'lemen."

"You're talking mighty big, black boy," Veldon said, "classing yourself with your betters. Drink the whiskey, and you can be the jester for the night."

The other men badgered and goaded Abe, but he stood his ground, his head high. A woman appeared

on the balcony at the end of the room and came down
the stairs with a stately tread. She wore a low-cut satin
gown, and jewels glittered on her powdered breast.
Her black hair was swept up in a smooth pompadour,
but neither the rouge nor the powder could hide the
ravages of time and dissipation on her angular face.

Tony remembered the woman, Nell Ambow. Five
years ago she had been less marked and coarsened by
her trade. Today she must be managing the girls. She
stopped halfway down the stairs and said sharply:

"Stop it! Stop horsing Abe! He has as much right to
be here as the rest of you saddle bums."

"Lay off, Nell. We're just having a little fun,"
Folger guffawed.

"We'll hold him," a couple of cowboys said, grab-
bing Abe. "You pour the redeye down, Blackie; we'll
hold him."

The two men caught Abe's arms and, struggle as he
would, his strength was no match for the two of them.
They pinioned his arms behind him. Another man
looped an arm around Abe's eyes and pulled his head
back. Blackie Folger snapped the cork from a bottle
and raised it to Abe's mouth.

Tony saw the liquor start to dribble from Abe's
thick lips, and then stark, cold reaction took over.
He was a victim of injustice, and it made every other
victim his brother. His slim white hand flashed like an
ivory shadow. The businesslike gun roared as it leveled,

and glass and whiskey sprayed across the struggling group.

The four men let go of Abe Jones. They whirled and crouched to face the brazen fool who had dared interfere with their deadly play. Their eyes scoured the room, none of them dreaming the thin, pale youth at the door could be the gunman. The gun was still smoking in Egan's hand, and comprehension dawned upon them with explosive force.

"A hayseed!" Folger roared. "An honest-to-goodness hayseed! You must be crazy, kid. Don't you know who I am?"

"You're white-livered cowards, all of you, ganging up on a man to make a jackass of him."

A deathly stillness closed about the room for a full minute. Folger rubbed his hand on his chaps and stood with his long legs slightly bent. A killer look came to his eyes.

"You shoot purty good with yore mouth, sodbuster. Anybody can bust a whiskey bottle with a bullet. Shooting at a man's different."

Tony knew that he had to stand his ground or crawl forever. The light in the saloon was none too bright, but it had glinted off the whiskey bottle, making it an easy target. He was in the shadows against the wall, while Folger was outlined against the lamps of the back-bar. He had to chance it. He slid his gun back into the holster, keeping his eyes on Folger.

"You want to try me, Blackie?" he said softly.

Death stood waiting, but Blackie Folger didn't move. One of the other men, with a forced laugh, broke the brittle stillness.

"Forget it, Blackie; we didn't come here for a killin'. We came to have some fun. The evening's just startin'. First things first, I say."

Nell Ambow had watched the play from the stairs; now she waved a jeweled hand at the room.

"Any more such horseplay, and I won't let the girls come down. The drinks are on the house."

A cowboy chortled, "You mean the drinks are on you, Nell. Dirkes will take the money out of your cut."

Abe Jones didn't retreat, despite his treatment. He bellied up to the bar, determined to earn his place among them. Nell descended the stairs and came directly to Tony.

"Who are you, pilgrim?" she asked in a grating voice.

"Brad Regan."

"You know what you just done?"

"Stopped a bad piece of business."

"Maybe. You also called out Blackie Folger and quailed him. He's top gun in these parts; or he was until now."

"Don't draw conclusions. Nothing's changed," Tony said quietly. "I was in the shadow; he was in the light."

"Your story. You had Blackie buffaloed, and you

know it. Take my advice and seek your entertainment somewhere else. Things will be uneasy as long as you're in the room. You won't get a hearty welcome at the Sabado Queen, but tell them Nell Ambow sent you to preserve the peace."

"Thank you, Nell. Sorry for the trouble."

"No trouble; you was right. Good night. And be careful."

Egan was conscious of the men staring at him as he went through the batwing door and into the black, cool night. Up the straight street he saw the Sabado Queen, less gaudy than the Red Garter and with carriage lights flanking the solid double doors. A number of carriages were parked around the big building and a few fancy saddle horses stood at the hitch rail.

Tony walked up to the white doors, turned the brass handle and walked inside. He closed the door and stopped a moment, marveling at the redecorating job Dirkes had done in the Sabado Queen. It showed the touch of a woman's hand, with its carpeted floor, the tapestries on the walls and the cut-glass chandeliers hanging on brass chains from the ceiling. The chairs at the tables that dotted the floor were upholstered in velvet, while the card games were shut off by a railing in one corner of the room.

There were women dressed in their Sunday best having a Saturday night on the town with their escorts or husbands. Tony realized at once that someone had made the place genteel to attract the trade from Holytown, as some people called it. The place was evidently reserved for businessmen, big ranchers, and mine owners who inhabited the territory. He doubted his welcome, but he walked up to the bar.

"You're in the wrong place, stranger," the barkeeper said. "The Red Garter is down the road a piece."

"I just came from there, mister. Nell Ambow asked me to leave to preserve the peace. She said to mention her name."

The barkeeper beckoned to one of the floor girls, who was dressed like a French maid. He whispered something to her, and she went to one of the tables. Tony's eyes followed her, and at the table he saw Carl Dirkes, dressed in broadcloth and white linen. He was talking to Bud Wilson, the rancher who needed a flunky. The maid said something to Carl, and he looked directly at Tony.

The floor girl came back to the bar. "Give him a drink and send him on his way; that's Dirkes' orders."

Tony felt his ears burn. "And what would your orders be, miss?"

The girl looked him up and down. "I'd have to mother you."

The bartender grinned and poured out a slug of whiskey. "I reckon," he said, "Dirkes let you have a drink because he can't make you out. A cowpoke he wouldn't cotton to, but a hayseed like you he might want to talk to. He's dead set against sodbusters getting a toe hold here."

Tony didn't answer him directly. His eyes were roving the back-bar as he sipped his drink slowly. His eyes brightened as he saw a guitar hanging on a peg in one corner. He had learned to play the guitar while in prison, and the warden had let him entertain the other inmates in the evening. His fingers tingled for the feel of the strings.

"That your guitar?" he asked the barkeeper.

"Heck, no, I wouldn't know one string from the other. It belonged to Singing Sam. He used to entertain here on Saturday nights."

"What do you mean, *used* to?"

"Got himself knifed in a brawl in a cantina across the border. Ain't nobody claimed the guitar yet. He's kinda missed around here; he had a soft crying voice."

A couple of ranchers came in and stood at the lower end of the bar. The barkeeper went to serve them, and Tony listened to the subdued voices in the room. The barkeeper came back to see that Tony finished his drink and got out.

"Could I hold that guitar a minute?" Tony asked.

"Think you can play it?"

"I can play some—not as good as Singing Sam, I'm sure," he hastened to add.

The barkeeper reluctantly took the guitar off the peg and handed it across the bar. Tony snugged it up to him and softly strummed the strings as he put it in tune. Then he stepped back a little, and the strings throbbed under his lean fingers.

There was a moment of stillness when the throbbing notes of the guitar died on the air. Then there was a burst of applause. The sudden acclamation took Tony by surprise. There were cries of, "More! More!" and dollars began rolling at his feet.

He picked up the money and stacked it on the bar. Then he held up his hand. He did not see the shadowy figure of the woman who came out on the balcony, summoned by the applause.

"Thank you kindly, folks," he said. "I had no notion of poking my nose into your evening. I was just trying out this guitar."

"Sing us another song!" a man yelled.

Even the early card players in the poker corner stopped to look his way as he sang an encore. More dollars rolled about his feet, and as he picked them up and put them on the bar he saw the woman coming down the stairs from the balcony. She spoke as she descended, a trace of asperity and malice in her voice.

"It looks as though I have some competition. Who is stirring you slugs to such impulsive admiration? You mean it's that hick at the bar?"

She continued to descend, and Dirkes got up quickly and went to take her hand.

"Just some innocent entertainment, my darling. The

boy wandered in. The crowd at the Red Garter were too tough for him," Dirkes said placatingly.

Dirkes took the woman's hand as she descended the last three steps. She was a proud woman, her head high, and her upswept hair was likely newly minted gold. Not until she moved under the glow of the chandeliers did Tony realize the truth.

The best kept woman in town! The woman on Dirkes' arm was Wilma Logan, his Wilma.

Wilma stopped in the center of the room and looked around, a stiff smile on her lips. She gave Tony a perfunctory, appraising glance before she spoke.

"Since you all seem to be so impatient for entertainment that you applaud a sodbuster, I have decided to start my entertainment early."

There was a ripple of applause. Dirkes, who had let go of her hand, frowned.

"Of course, my dear. But Hal Mendel, the piano man, hasn't come yet. He didn't expect you to start early."

There was an awkward pause, and then some devil deep inside of him made Egan speak up. He even managed a whimsical smile.

"I reckon I can strum along with you, ma'am, if you're so minded," he offered.

Wilma looked at him, his cheap boots, his bib overalls, his cotton shirt and slouch hat. Then she threw back her head and laughed uncontrollably.

"Why not?" she said. "We can split the money they

throw at you."

"Just trying to be helpful, Mrs. Dirkes," he said, unperturbed, hoping she would deny the name he used. There was no denial.

"Take your hat off, yokel," she said. "Come on back to the piano. This might prove to be a diversion; Hal is a lousy pianist."

Balancing his hat on the brass footrail in front of the bar, he followed her. When she stopped and faced the room, Tony took a position behind her.

"You start, Mrs. Dirkes," he used the name again deliberately, "and I'll pick you up."

Wilma drew herself up, clasped her hands in front of her and began to sing "The Old Oaken Bucket." Egan picked up the chord immediately, as this was one of the songs they had sung together in prison to his accompaniment. The crowd was quiet as her voice lifted in plaintive song. She was no Jenny Lind—her voice was too deep and not quite true—but it had a husky quality that made every word sound sincere. The guitar added just enough beat to liven the music, which pleased the untrained audience. The applause was unrestrained, but no silver dollars cart-wheeled about their feet. She went into "The Camptown Races" and "I Dream of Jeanie With The Light Brown Hair," standards that did not tax Tony's skill.

When the concert was over and the applause had died down, Tony was no richer for his assistance. He took the guitar back to the bartender, expecting to be evicted from the place now that the entertainment was over. As he passed the guitar over the bar and pocketed the dollars he had stacked there, he heard a sharp exchange of words between Wilma and Carl Dirkes. He turned around and saw that, instead of sitting in the chair Dirkes had reserved for her, Wilma was heading for the stairs.

"Where are you going, honey?" Dirkes said, his voice stern in spite of the endearment. "We expected you to sit here with us."

"I'm going upstairs to my room for a while," she said evenly.

"You were just up there. I'll send one of the girls for anything you need."

"I'm sorry, Carl," Wilma retorted; "she couldn't find what I'm looking for."

It could have been the uncertain light, but Tony was startled by what he thought was a glint of venomous hate in her eyes. It was evident that Dirkes was incensed as he watched her climb regally up the stairs.

Tony had just picked up his hat from the brass foot-rail when Dirkes spoke to him.

"Come here, stranger." The words were an order.

As docile as the sodbuster he resembled, Tony went to the table where Bud Wilson sat with Dirkes. Wilson had a woman with him.

"What's your name?" Dirkes asked, his flat face

unmoving.

"His name's Brad Regan," Wilson put in. "He's going to flunky for me on my spread."

"Not so fast, Bud," Dirkes said. "So you're Brad Regan, eh?"

"You heard him right."

"You look mighty white and underfed to me. What prison did you just get out of?"

Tony tensed. "I don't recollect mentioning any prison."

"You sang a prison song."

"I picked it up from a feller up at the mining camps. I'm a hardrock miner. The dark and damp don't do much for a man's skin, and the bad air and hard work ain't exactly fattening."

"You ever been in Sabado before?"

"Just to ride through."

"How about singing here on Saturday nights? Wilson will give you time off."

"I'm not Wilson's man yet. I told him I'd have to think about it. Besides, I can't work here. Your wife resents me, Mr. Dirkes."

"Wilma has to be top dog, but she'll get used to the idea. After all, you're different kinds of entertainers. You won't cause any trouble."

Egan winced. Cause any trouble? Trouble was the only thing he intended to cause, but in his own way and his own time. First he wanted some answers.

"I'll think on it, sir," Egan said obsequiously. "Do I have to get out of here now?"

"Suit yourself. I guess you made your way in with the customers."

"Would they let me sit in on a poker game?"

"You'll lose your shirt."

Tony jingled the money in his jeans. "I got this money here; I might as well leave it here."

"You don't impress me as either a sodbuster or a miner," Dirkes said, frowning. "If you want to lose your shirt, it's up to you." Dirkes raised his voice and shouted across the room. "Hey, Barney, this singing kid wants to sit in on a game. He's hankering to lose the money he scrabbled off the floor."

"Send him over. Singing won't get him far here."

Seated at one of the card tables under a hanging light, Tony felt a thrill of anticipation go through him. He and Patch had bucked some hard games in their bounty-hunting days, and in prison he had not spent all his leisure time singing.

"Give the pilgrim the deal," one man said, chuckling. "He'll probably be broke before he gets another chance at it."

Tony, without comment, took the deck and tried to be a little awkward in shuffling them, but his trained fingers felt for any imperfections. He was satisfied it was an honest deck.

"Jacks or better," he said, doling out the cards.

The bet was checked around to him. He picked up his cards and saw that he had a nine, ten, jack and two queens. His cards were of the same suit, diamonds, except for the odd queen of spades. He opened on the strength of his queens, and then he split his queens to make a try for the straight flush. He showed his openers before discarding. He shuffled the queens in his hand so the others would not know his discard. They might easily think that, being green, he would draw for another queen.

He dealt the cards. Finney, a tall thin man who owned the furniture store and undertaking business in Holytown and who was a deacon in the church, took one card. Tony figured he was either bluffing or taking a long chance. Tony knew the players or had heard of them. Most of them were pillars of society on Sundays, but Saturday night belonged to the devil. He dealt Ballard, the butcher, two cards. Deadmer—Dr. Deadmer took none. Tony dropped himself a card, the eight of diamonds. He had hit a straight flush, but he didn't bat an eye. As opener he had the first bet, and he made it a modest one.

The betting went around, Finney raising at each turn. Tony realized that he had drawn only one card, the same number as Finney, but it was doubtful they both had drawn just the right card. Either Finney had four of a kind or he was bluffing. Tony calculated his money. He had picked up twenty dollars off the floor, and he had had six of his prison dole. He had already put eight dollars in the pot. He decided he might not have such a good hand for a long time, so next time around he called Finney and raised him.

"I reckon I'll bet the rest of my pile," he said blandly, shoving in his last twelve dollars.

Ballard dropped out. Finney cackled.

"I reckon you want to die fast, boy. Well, I'm the man who can bury you."

Finney shoved in twelve dollars with a confident grin. Doc dropped out, so Tony turned up his cards, a straight flush. Finney had already flipped his cards over, showing a straight, and was already scraping in the pot.

"Hold it, sir," Tony said politely. "You ain't read my cards right."

Ballard guffawed. "The kid has a straight flush, Finney. You better put off the burying you spoke of."

Finney gawked at Tony's cards and looked up at Tony with puckered eyes. "Beginner's luck," he grumbled.

Tony lost a couple of small pots and then began to win consistently. He played quietly, with concentration, but the other three men became restless at the knowledge the sodbuster was taking them. They called for a new deck, which suited Tony fine. The rest of the bar was filling up. Mendel the pianist had come, and couples were dancing to his music. Then a buffet was served at one end of the bar, and the men were filling plates for the ladies, or asking the French maids to do so.

Tony felt the pangs of hunger returning. He now had over two hundred dollars in front of him.

The next hand Finney dealt. When Tony picked up his cards, he accidentally dropped a trey of clubs. Finney saw it, and so did the others, but Tony picked it up without asking for a new deal. Finney smirked and finished the deal.

"Check here," Doc Deadmer said.

Tony spread his cards so he could just read the numbers. He had two deuces and a pair of treys. He could have opened on the two pairs, but he chose not to.

"Check," he said flatly.

Finney gave him a shrewd look. "I'll open for five dollars," he said, after Ballard checked.

The doctor stayed, and the bet came to Tony. "I'll raise you five," he said, tossing in ten dollars.

"What kind of poker you playing, pilgrim?" Finney snapped. "You just checked. Now you raise."

"It's ethical," Ballard grumbled, tossing in ten dollars. "I reckon the greenhorn ain't as green as he appears."

In his turn Tony discarded his odd card, knowing the odds against filling his full house were eleven to one. It was time to take a chance while he was playing with their money. They all gave him curious glances. Finney snorted.

"How come you drawing only one card?"

"Play your hand, Finney; I'll play mine." That time Tony had forgotten to say "sir."

Finney stood pat. Tony looked at his draw card and felt a thrill he tried to conceal. He had made it—drawn a deuce. He had a full house. The betting went around the table. Tony raised twice, and Ballard dropped out on the second raise. Doc Deadmer raised the time around, indicating he had a top hand or was bluffing. Tony called him, but Finney confidently raised again. Finney had to have four of a kind or a straight flush to beat him, and the odds against being dealt such a pat hand were fifty to one. On the next bet Tony made his play, after the doctor had decided he had had enough.

"I'll raise a hundred," he said, passing the bet to Finney.

There was a moment of tense silence at the table. There was something about this kid that didn't shape up. Either he had the luck of the damned, or he was not the pilgrim he appeared.

"I'll see you," Finney said, drawing in his breath. He put up his money and turned his cards, an ace high straight. He stood looking at Tony like a hawk.

Deliberately Tony put his card down, announcing, "Full house, treys and deuces."

Finney stared at the small cards, realizing they beat his straight. His face flushed biliously, and his lips curled as he snarled:

"You come here parading as a pilgrim and trick us

out of our money!"

Tony heard the words, fighting words. He kept his hands on the table one second too long. Finney had snatched a small gun from somewhere in his black broadcloth and opened fire point-blank.

Tony felt a club smash his head; smash him to the floor.

CHAPTER THREE

Wilma Dirkes sat at her dressing table in her room off the balcony, her head buried on her arms, when she heard the shot. It came through the thin walls like the pop of a firecracker. She stiffened. No shooting was tolerated in the Sabado Queen since she had come there. She rose quickly and ran out on the balcony. She couldn't see the corner that held the card tables until she was on the stairs. She saw the men milling there.

"What happened?" she asked in a sharp, clear voice.

A man looked up at her, his face excited. "The pilgrim has been shot!" he called out.

"What do you mean?" She couldn't believe her ears.

Carl Dirkes turned from the card table where the commotion was and saw her.

"I'll handle it, my dear; don't let it disturb you."

"But he's been shot!" she retorted. "Is he dead?"

"I don't know."

In her satin dress and jewels, Wilma ran down the

stairs. She reached the group, avoiding Carl's hand that tried to hold her back. Pushing through the crowd, she saw the sodbuster lying there with blood oozing from his head. She stooped quickly, examining the wound, unmindful of the blood on her fingers. She took his pulse, half hearing the commotion about her.

"You had no call to shoot him, Finney," Ballard said.

"What do you mean—no cause? Must a man sit still and be robbed?"

Dr. Deadmer said, "We robbed ourselves. We misjudged him. He outsmarted us, that's all."

"He cheated, he must have cheated," Finney said, beside himself with guilty anger.

"They were our cards, not his. He looked like a pilgrim, but he knew the game better than we did."

Carl came over and faced Finney. "You know the rules here, Finney; no cheating and no shooting. Get out and don't come back here."

"But, Carl, a man has a right—"

"Shut up and get out! A poor loser who blames his mistakes on another is no excuse for a man. Get out or I'll throw you out!"

"I want my money back," Finney whined.

Wilma stood up and looked at Finney with utter contempt. "The money stays. You go."

Finney picked up his hat and jammed it on his head. Running the gauntlet of scorn, he made his way to the door with murder in his heart.

"Take the kid up to my room," Wilma ordered the men. "Somebody bring his winnings along."

She led the way up the stairs, followed by Bud Wilson, who carried Tony in his arms as though he were a child. Carl followed, bringing Tony's money off the table.

"Get back to your fun," Carl said. "The drinks are on the house."

Wilson laid Tony on Wilma's bed. Dr. Deadmer, who had come upstairs after Carl, took charge.

"Put the money on my dressing table and take his boots off, Carl," Wilma ordered.

The doctor turned to Wilma. "Bring me some water in the basin, and some clean cloths if you have any."

Wilma poured water from the pitcher and put the basin near the bed. She took out a linen petticoat and proceeded to tear it up.

"You and Wilson go downstairs and keep things going," she said to Carl. "The doctor and I can take care of the boy."

Along with the doctor, Wilma watched as he washed the wound. She saw him stop and look at the boy's face for a long time. He rubbed his finger over the skin on the cheeks.

"What's the matter?" she asked.

"The bullet creased him. He's unconscious. Only time can tell whether he'll come out of it or not."

"Why were you rubbing his face?"

"The skin looks so unnatural. He has some scars hidden in the hair on the side of his head. He must have had a head injury before."

"His skin is white and so smooth," Wilma said.

"I heard him say he has been working in the mines. The mines can do that to a man, and worse. They can eat out his lungs. There's nothing more we can do for him now but wait."

"You go on down and enjoy yourself, Doctor. I'll sit with him for a while. If I need you, I'll call."

When the doctor had gone, Wilma studied the white face on the bed. The doctor had not even bothered to bandage the wound, as the bleeding had stopped. Silently she prayed that he would regain consciousness. She went to the dressing table and counted his money. Many of the bets above twenty dollars had been made in gold. All in all, there were four hundred and twenty dollars in the stacks of gold and silver.

She reached into the bottom drawer of her dressing table and took out a small book. Opening the book, she wrote with concentration for a minute or so. Then she closed the book, put it in the bottom drawer and locked the drawer. She was unaware of Tony watching her from the bed.

"Where am I?" he asked in a voice that sounded far away.

Wilma rose quickly and came to the bed, concern in her violet eyes. She brushed back a stray lock of her gold hair, and when her face was within focus, Egan knew he had never seen anything more beautiful.

"Who are you?" He knew who she was, but he dared not admit it.

"I'm Wilma Dirkes. You played for me while I sang down in the barroom."

"I remember now. I was singing, and you came down and took over."

"It was a catty thing to do, pilgrim. I apologize. I'm not a real woman any more; I'm a front for Carl Dirkes. I'm jealous of everyone because I hate myself. I worked to be top lady in this scummy town for one purpose. Nobody knows my purpose, but they will when it's accomplished."

"I don't know, Mrs. Dirkes; the paper gave a good account of you. You help people. Just like now, you're helping me. How did I get here?"

"You were shot in a card game."

"Did they take my money?"

"No. It's over here. I counted it—four hundred and twenty dollars. Maybe the shot was a stroke of fate. If you had gone out into the street with that much money, you might have waked up with a knife in your back. Finney wasn't very happy when he left here."

Tony closed his eyes and felt the throbbing pain in his head. He had made a pretty good record for one night; Folger and Finney both had a score to settle with him.

"How is your head, sonny?" She put a cool, smooth hand on his brow.

"It hurts like blazes." The name "Sonny" amused him.

"An inch closer and you'd be dead. What's your name?"

"Brad—Brad Regan. Where am I?"

"You're in my room at the Sabado Queen."

"I got no right here. I'd better scramble."

"You could become unconscious again, you know. That bullet dug a furrow. You had better stay flat on your back," Wilma told him.

He pushed her hand away. "I can't stay in your room," he said firmly.

He stood up, and the room spun around him. A black film came over his eyes, and pain shot through his head. He fell back on the costly counterpane.

"Are you satisfied?" Wilma chastised him. "You're not a strong man at best. How did you get so frail and white?"

Tony was silent for a moment, waiting for the throbbing of his head to subside. If Dr. Deadmer had examined his wound, he might have suspected the truth about the plastic surgery, and if he had he might have conveyed his suspicions to Wilma.

"What did the doctor say?" he hazarded.

"He said you had been working in the mines. He said the mines could bleach and choke a man to death."

"He said true." Few doctors knew about this new surgery.

"Why don't you come to work for Carl and me? I could fatten you up."

That would be purgatory, watching Carl put his hands on her, watching her driving with Carl, eating with Carl. It was doubtful he could retain his sanity or his identity under such conditions.

"I have a job," he said flatly.

"Doing what?"

"I'm going to flunky for the cook at Bud Wilson's ranch."

Wilma looked at him with annoyance, her lips pursed. "I suppose that's all you're fit for."

Her annoyance irked him. "Why should my doings concern you, Mrs. Dirkes?"

"Call me Wilma. They don't concern me, but a lad who can sing like you did tonight and beat three of the best at poker might aim higher."

"A man's got to start some place."

"Lay there and rest. I've got to go downstairs, or Carl will be up here after me."

"Where will you sleep?"

"We stay here Saturday nights, as Carl plays cards until near morning. We go from here directly to church. I'll sleep in Carl's room tonight."

Her words cut Tony, but he tried to overlook them.

"Will I see you again tonight?" he asked.

"You had better sleep; that is your best medicine. I'll see you in the morning."

She was gone, and Tony lay there, wondering at the macabre hand Fate had dealt him.

He drifted off to sleep, fatigued by the weird events of the day. When he awoke he had no idea what time it was. The lamp on the dressing table was turned low; she had been there. The pain in his head had subsided, and he swung his feet to the floor. Standing up, he discovered that the dizziness had all but gone. The place was quiet. Walking to the dressing table, he turned up the lamp and looked at his watch. It was four-thirty in the morning.

His money was gone, and he wondered what had become of it. He doubted that Wilma had appropriated it for her own use, and he doubted that anybody would have the audacity to enter her room even if it were unlocked. He thought of the drawer he had seen her lock after putting the book away. He had to get his money and get out of there before anybody was up. To remain so close to Wilma and Carl Dirkes was to risk the detection of his real identity. He knelt down and examined the lock of the drawer. Pulling out his pocketknife, he forced the small blade into the crack at the top of the door and slid the bolt down. The drawer opened quietly.

His money was inside, tied in a kerchief. Lifting the money out, he spied the book she had been writing in the night before. He lifted the book and held it under the lamplight. He had no compunction about reading the contents.

Staring at the open book, he was startled at what was recorded there. It was as complete and damning as the ledger of Saint Peter at the golden gate. There were dates and amounts of robberies. There were entries of cattle stolen. There were accounts of murders, and the first account in the book was that of his conviction over five years before. Why had Wilma kept such a record? Did she hope to use it as a club over Dirkes should he ever threaten or oppose her? There were no names in the book; just the dates, the description of the crime and the probable returns. He put the book back into the drawer, and, finding a piece of paper, scribbled a note to Wilma thanking her for her care and apologizing for opening the drawer. This he put in the drawer on top of the book. Then he held the bolt down until it was under the keeper and shoved the drawer in until the bolt clicked home.

He couldn't chance going out through the barroom, because the door would be locked and the swamper might be busy obliterating the filth of the evening's fun. Outside the window, the first gray light of dawn was showing. The window was already raised to let in the cool night air and, looking out, he discovered the roof of the lean-to kitchen just under the window sill. He put on his boots, his hat and gunbelt, and stuffing the kerchief of money in the front of his shirt, climbed over the sill to the kitchen roof. At the end of the kitchen was a storage shed with a lower roof, so that he was able to drop the last few feet to the ground.

Reaching the livery barn, he left some money on the counter behind which the stable man was sleeping off his own private Saturday night. He saddled his crow-bait and rode out the deserted streets and alleys of Honkytown. He regretted that it was Sunday and the stores would be closed so that he could not buy himself a decent outfit of clothes and make a trade for a better horse. He rode around the upper part of town to the cottonwoods that lined the creek. Here he washed his face, combed his hair with the stub of a comb he carried and waited until he thought Lupe would be starting early breakfast.

He tied his horse in front of Lupe's Café and turned to stare at Ruby Miller's shop next door. He wondered how Ruby had spent Saturday night. She lived in two rooms behind her shop, or she had lived there when she had been Patch Roger's girl and they had been planning on the house they would build on the ranch Patch was homesteading. He entered the café and sat at the counter.

"You *mucho* early, *Señor* Brad. You no *celebrar* the *sabado* last night?"

"Lupe," Tony grinned, "I had a right peaceable time. Went to bed early."

Her sharp eyes saw the still red crease on the side of his head. "You have the fight last night?"

"No fight, Lupe. I bumped my head."

"On the bullet?"

"I'm a peaceable man, as I said before. Give me some hot cakes."

"Hot cakes for peegs. I breen you *desayuno* for a man."

"I reckon your breakfast will be all right, Lupe."

Lupe disappeared into the kitchen. A couple came in and sat at one of the tables. Not all the people of Sabado were roisterers. Another couple with a child came in, dressed in their Sunday best. Lupe came out and took their orders, then went to the kitchen and returned with Tony's breakfast: steak, eggs, and hash-browned potatoes. Tony looked at his plate and smiled.

"So that's a man's breakfast. Do I get coffee this morning?"

Lupe gave him a motherly look, shaking a finger at him. "You don't *apreciar* what I do for you." She poured him a cup of coffee.

Tony, having had nothing to eat since noon of the day before, savored the meal, and he was halfway through his steak when Ruby Miller came in. Without hesitation Ruby took the stool beside him. Tony, surprised, smiled at her.

"What's the matter, Ruby; can't you stand your own food any more?"

Her brown eyes studied him, and he felt nervous under her scrutiny.

"What do you know about my cooking, sodbuster? Who are you, anyway?"

"I told you. Brad Regan, and no sodbuster."

"Sodbuster or not, you seem to have made quite an impression on Honkytown. Only a fool would brace Blackie Folger with a gun, but it would take a smart man to best Finney, Ballard and Dr. Deadmer at cards. You look like neither."

"How do you know what happened in Honkytown? Were you there?"

"News like that travels fast. I also heard that you found Wilma."

"I found her. Your description of her was fitting. Best kept woman in town."

"I heard she made a fuss over you. You have three reasons for leaving Sabado before it gets over its hangover: Folger, Finney, and Dirkes. You passed out the grudges real liberally. My advice is for you to get lost. This town gobbles up greenhorns, smart alecks and weaklings." Her voice was bitter.

"Are you bitter because you can't get a man?" he jibed her.

Her eyes dropped. "I've got a man."

"But he's not the man you want?" Tony pressed her. "He doesn't compare with some man you had in the past, is that it?"

"Why should you pry into my life?" She got up and went to one of the tables.

Tony realized her reason for sitting next to him was to give him a warning. Why she would want to warn him he didn't know. He finished his breakfast and went outside.

Tony mounted and turned his horse toward the Tall-W. He did not have to ask the way.

CHAPTER FOUR

Tony's advent on the Tall-W was without incident. Some of the men had seen the gunplay in the bar, and all of them heard of the card game at the Sabado Queen. They jibed him about it but with a bewildered respect. He learned one other thing: Abe Jones was horse wrangler on the spread. Abe took him aside after supper the first night.

"Ah'm plumb grateful for what you'all done last night, Pahdner. Howsomeeveh, a man got to earn his own respect. If he don't whimper an' crawl, they gits tihed of wuppin' him. You made yo s'elf a enemy, man. I ain't fohgittin' whyfoh."

He had a talk with Wilson, too. Wilson called him up to the big house, where Wilson lived with his wife and their son and daughter. Bud Wilson was a man who thought himself just, and he had the good grace to introduce Tony to his family, who were seated about the large living room reading.

"This is Brad Regan," he announced.

Tony in turn met Mrs. Wilson, a woman marked by the hard work of starting a ranch in the wilderness. She was thin and drawn, with a natural graciousness and reserve. He met Lucy Wilson, a round-faced girl with flashing eyes and a mop of hair cut almost as shot as a boy's. He judged her to be sixteen. He met Kent, the son, a tall boy of seventeen or so with his father's features but not yet gone to fat. His eyes had a suspicious look, and he seemed to be balancing a chip on his shoulder.

"Do you think you can carry a platter of side meat, kid?" Kent remarked, shaking hands reluctantly.

"Don't mind him," Wilson said. "He figures every man who comes here is going to keep him from ramrodding this outfit. When he gets dry behind the ears, he'll know that ramrodding is a man's job, and a ramrod with a chip on his shoulder ain't worth his salt."

Kent's face turned pink and his jaw stiffened. Tony knew that Wilson's words were worse than a spanking to a kid that age. Seventeen was a nothing age, a pause between a boy and a man. He tried to ease the boy's chagrin.

"I reckon a man learns as he grows. Ain't none of us born smart."

"Would you care for some tea?" Mrs. Wilson said.

"Tea?" Wilson echoed. "Keep that for your ladies' aid society, Kate. This ranny is tougher than he looks.

"Come into my office, boy."

In the square, meagerly furnished room, Wilson lit the lamp and turned to him. Tony sat down, wondering what was coming.

"I like what I hear about you, boy."

"What did you hear?"

"You faced down Blackie Folger. Is that right?"

"I was in the shadow; he was in the lamp glare. It wasn't a fair try."

"I like modesty. You *did* dare him and he didn't draw, right?"

"That's the way it's told."

"Where did you learn to throw a gun like that?"

"Just funnin' around. I knew a saloon swamper who could outdraw any man that walks, but he doesn't work at it."

"That's a dangerous pastime, Brad. You don't fun with a man like Folger. You're tailor-made for a job I have in mind. Would you like to hear about it?"

"Listening never done a man harm, Mr. Wilson."

"Call me Bud like the rest of the boys do. I'm losing stock, not in big bunches, but in little dribbles. I've got four men working for me beside Abe, the wrangler. I don't like to accuse any of them of bleeding me, because they might be innocent. Someone else could have a pipe line to my herd."

"You want me to spy for you. Is that it?"

"What's wrong with that?"

"I'm not selling my gun."

"I'm not buying your gun, but being able to use your gun will be an asset in case you get cornered."

"I hired out to flunky."

"That's the good part of it. You will flunky, but you need exercise to put meat on your bones; you need sunshine to brown your skin. You flunky the breakfast; then you're off until supper. It takes you say two hours a meal to put the food on the table, clear it off, and wash the dishes. Add a half-hour to sweep out the bunkhouse. In between you ride where you please on the range."

"I've got a crow-bait horse."

"Abe will cut you out a horse from the remuda."

Tony began to see the advantage of the setup.

"I'll give it a try," he agreed, "but I'll want to buy my horse."

"Pick any one you want for thirty dollars. I'll take it out of your pay."

"I'd rather pay cash and get a bill of sale. I don't want to be cornered for a horse thief and strung up before you can back my word."

"Have it your way."

Tony pulled the kerchief of money out of his shabby hat. He had transferred it there from the front of his shirt on entering the house. He doled out a gold piece and ten silver dollars.

"You can leave a space for the description of the

horse to be filled in after I make my pick."

Bud grunted, "You're fast and smart and careful. You sure you're not up to something?"

"Just trying to make out, Bud. You got a safe?"

Bud nodded to the iron box in the shadows in one corner of the room. "You ain't real trusting, are you, Brad?"

"It depends. I'm trusting you to put my money in your safe and keep it for me. Ain't no sense in throwing temptation in the way of honest men."

When the money was put away, Tony went back to the bunkhouse.

After sweeping out the bunkhouse in the morning, he hunted up Abe Jones down at the corrals.

"Mohnin', son," Abe greeted him, "Bud said you was to have the pick of the remuda."

"I'd rather not have *my* pick, Abe," Tony countered.

"Why foh yo'all talk lak that?"

"I'll take your pick, Abe. You know the remuda; I don't."

"Me, ah'd take that gray gelding ovah yondah. He's got a deep chest, good for wind; long loins and low withers make for a strong back. Man, look at them long legs. He's a foh-year-old; got his full strength."

Tony approved the choice.

"That one will do, Abe. What's he called?"

"Extrano—reckon it means stranger in Spanish. Miss Lucy named him."

Tony frowned. He was a stranger, too, a stranger in his own land.

"Why did she name him that?"

"Ah reckon 'cause he jest drifted in with the remuda one day. He's still a slick. I figgah he come from one of them wild herds, but he wasn't wild. Bein' a gelding, he wasn't after no mares. I figgah he drifted away from a wagon train or escaped from some Indian fight."

"Does Lucy claim him?"

"Them kids claim everything on the Tall-W. You stay here a week, an' they might try to put a brand on yo'." Abe laughed, showing his white teeth.

"I'll take him."

"Yo'all want to brand him with yoah mahk?"

His mark? What was his mark? He and Patch had had a brand when they had started with the wild cows they had dug out of the Texas chaparral. It was an R with an E backward on the front of the R. The brand would still be known around there.

"I wouldn't burn his beautiful hide, Abe. But I'll brand him. Can you rope him and hold him down?"

"Sho' 'nuff, Brad."

"Bring him to the blacksmith shop."

At the blacksmith shop, Tony heated a heavy wire in the forge until it was white hot. Abe brought the gray horse and got him to lie down without too much difficulty. He sat on the horse's head.

"Hold his ear for me, Abe. This won't hurt him

much."

Inside the ear he carefully branded an E.

Abe let the horse up. "Why foah you put that E theah? Youah names' Brad Regan."

Tony couldn't reveal his real name, not even to Abe. "Let's just say the E stands for excellence, Abe."

"Ah got a good extra saddle I won in a poker game, Brad. It's youahs."

"I'll buy it from you."

"I'm beholden to you'all now. You jest ride that saddle in good health."

Tony didn't argue. He knew that a man considered a favor a burden until it was returned. Saddling up, he rode the gray up to the big house and went in to have Wilson fill in the description of the horse on the bill of sale. Wilson looked out the window.

"You also know horseflesh, amongst your other assets, Brad. I got a hunch you ain't a hardrock miner or a sodbuster. There's one other likelihood."

"Does it matter, Boss?" Tony asked stiffly.

Wilson looked at him closely. "Not as long as you do your job. A man's past is his own."

"I'm off to do that job, Wilson," Tony said, turning to go. Wilson had guessed close to the truth—jailbird. In the yard, he found Lucy Wilson petting Extrano. She looked up at him, shaking the wild hair out of her eyes.

"You're free with other people's belongings, aren't

you?"

"What do you mean by that, Lucy?"

"Extrano is my horse. I named him."

"Abe says you claim them all. Yore paw gave me my choice; this is it."

"I'll loan him to you, Brad Regan," she said gravely.

"I've got a bill of sale duly signed and receipted," Tony said.

"Let *me* give him to you, then. That way *you'll* owe *me*."

"You drive a hard bargain, Lucy," Tony grinned and, mounting, rode away.

He was late getting back, and his chores in the kitchen needed tending to. He donned his apron in the warm kitchen, which smelled of roasting meat and boiling vegetables. He set the dishes and cutlery on the long table, filled the water pitchers and brought in the stacks of bread. Chow Lee filled the bowls with the pungent food, and Tony set them out at intervals along the table. Then he went out and banged on the triangle that was hanging on the porch.

Tony ate after the other men were through, as he had to wait on the table, and Chow Lee, the bustling little Chinese, broiled him a special steak so rare it looked almost raw.

When the dishes were washed, he went directly to the bunkhouse. The inevitable card game had already started, and the men made a place for him.

"Abe tells us you were out riding today, Brad," Baudry said, studying his cards.

"Wilson gave me permission," Tony said, picking up his own cards.

"See anything out of the way?"

Tony realized that was a leading question and took the bait. "I saw the doggonedest thing. I rode beyond the line fence across the barranca."

"You mean onto Dirkes' range?"

"Is that his range?" Tony asked innocently.

"Shore is. He ain't one to take kindly to trespassers. If I was you, I would keep out of there."

"I didn't mean no harm."

"You can't argue with a bullet, boy. What was this doggonedest thing you seen?"

'I'll open the pot for a dime," Simpson said. He was a white-headed Swede with a raw-boned body.

"I'll stay," said a short meaty man called "Fats."

Tony threw in his nickel, as did Bengo, the heavy-set man on his left. Bengo had a swarthy skin and sharp black eyes.

"What was it you seen?" Baudry insisted, making his bet.

"I seen twenty-five head of Tall-W cattle on Dirkes' range. Funny thing was I couldn't figure how they got through the drift fence; there was no wire down."

"I'll draw three, said Simpson, who was evidently holding a pair.

"Make mine two," Fats said, licking his thick lips.

Tony looked at his cards. He had two pairs and an ace. He decided to stand pat, knowing he had an eleven to one chance of bettering his hand. Simpson, who was dealing, gave him a sharp look. Bengo took one card and Baudry took two.

"What did you do about the cattle?" Baudry asked.

Tony shrugged. "I herded them back on Tall-W range."

Baudry almost dropped his cards. "You what?"

"I found a splice in the drift fence, and I took down the wires. I shoved the cows a good piece inside Wilson's grass."

Baudry jiggled his cards around. His head jerked up. "Did you report that to Wilson?"

"I figured there was no need to. I got the cows back."

"You could have been shot dead, taking cows off Box-X range," Bengo said, studying his cards.

Tony grinned. "Well, I didn't get shot."

"Did you see anybody with the cattle?"

"I saw two men from a distance, but I don't know if they was with the cattle or not. One was riding a bay horse and the other a sorrel."

"You hintin' them cattle were rustled?"

"I didn't say that; you did."

"Next you'll be namin' names. I ride a bay horse; Fats rides a sorrel."

"Were you on Box-X today?"

"No."

"Then it couldn't have been you, could it?"

"Let's play cards," Simpson said impatiently. "I bet a dime."

Fats called him. Tony bet the dime and raised fifteen cents.

"Two-bits is the limit," Baudry said.

"I know it," Tony replied.

Bengo folded and so did Baudry. Simpson called and lay down his cards as Fats folded. Simpson had two pairs identical with Tony's, but Tony's ace won him the pot.

The game went on. In a pause to roll smokes, Baudry said, "I don't savvy you, kid. You look like a puny yokel, yet you flash a gun, play cards, and stick your nose in range business like a rannie born to prosper. Are you fronting for somebody?"

"Just myself. I aim to make me a stake any way I can."

"That's touchy talk, Regan. Finney ain't through with that poker game you played him yet. He could get his money back in payment for your funeral."

"I ain't never yet seen a poor loser who was a hero," Tony said blandly.

"I'm goin' outside for a smoke. Want to come along?"

Mystified but alert, Tony said, "Sure thing."

Tony followed Baudry to the rear of the bunkhouse, where Baudry carefully rolled a quirly. The moon was nearly full, and the buildings and sheds of the Tall-W stood out in the silver light. Baudry waved his hand around.

"How would you like to own a piece of this spread?" he asked without preliminaries.

"I lost you. Come again."

"You're not a fool, Regan. I got a notion you're a hombre with plenty savvy. You're not foolin' me none. You saw Fats and me push them cattle onto Box-X. I'm giving you a chance to be a live friend instead of a dead witness. Keep your mouth shut, play along with us, and you're in."

"Come again. I don't buy half a deal. How you goin' to steal Wilson's herd in dribbles? His increase will take care of that."

"You can start a lake with a drop of water. We plant enough cattle on Dirkes' range, botch the brand blotting, and leak the news to Wilson. Him and Dirkes get along for mutual protection, but they ain't in love with each other. We start a range war between Dirkes and Wilson, and when they cut each other down to size, we step in."

"Who's back of this deal? You got to have somebody on the other side of the fence."

"Sure we have; he's ramroddin' the deal. It will get you off the hook with him. He wouldn't call out a friend."

"Name me a name."

"Blackie Folger. He's back of it. We push the cattle over the line a few head at a time; he takes care of botching the brands without Dirkes knowing it. Fats and me need some help. Nobody would suspect you of rustling."

"Why are you telling me all this, Baudry? I didn't say I was in yet."

"You're in or you're dead."

"All right," Tony said grimly. "I'm in."

CHAPTER FIVE

After washing the breakfast dishes in the morning and sweeping out the bunkhouse, Tony went to the blacksmith shop where Abe Jones was shoeing a horse.

"Mawnin', Brad," Abe greeted him, dropping his hammer to the clanging anvil.

"Mornin', Abe. Will you do me a favor?"

"You knows I will, Brad."

"Go up to the big house when you finish with the horse, and tell Mr. Wilson to meet me on the range about a mile from here where that spring comes out from some high rocks."

"Why you don' tell him yo'self?"

"I've got my reasons."

He did have his reasons. Baudry wasn't going to take him on trust right off; he might be spying to see if he went to the big house.

"Ah'll sho' nuff do what you want, pardner, but ain't Mr. Wilson goin' to think it kinda odd?"

"Tell him it's important. Another thing, Abe: don't tell anybody about this. It could get me in bad trouble."

"Lawsy no, man, I won't breathe it to a soul."

"Not even to his family. Lucy and Kent are already after my hide."

With Abe's solemn promise to be discreet, Tony mounted his gray gelding and took off into the hot sun. He took a roundabout trail, making sure he wasn't being followed. When he reached the spring gurgling from the earth within its haven of high rocks, he composed himself to wait. He wasn't sure he was doing the right thing, but he had to chance it.

Bud Wilson arrived about an hour after Tony had begun his vigil. Wilson had a concerned look on his face.

"What's all this secrecy, Regan?"

"I don't rightly know how to tell you this, sir. I went riding up to the northwest corner of your range yesterday, and I saw something mighty peculiar."

"So?"

Tony explained in detail just what had happened the day before. He ended up with Baudry's proposition and ultimatum.

"You sure got fast results on the spying job I gave you, but are you sure you aren't jumping to conclusions?"

Tony frowned. "What do you mean by that?"

"Instead of Dirkes trying to pick a fight with me, I could be trying to pick a fight with him."

"You mean you're deliberately shoving beef on Dirkes' range? That ain't the way Baudry told it."

"Baudry could be trying to get you into trouble. Suppose you faced Blackie Folger and said he was back of the rustling? And suppose he called you a liar?"

"You mean gunplay?"

"Folger is going to have to face you after the way you cowed him; that or leave the country. Every man around here knows that, and they could be making bets on the outcome right now."

"That can wait. I'll face Folger when and if he forces it. How about this rustling bit? Are you leveling with me?"

"Not exactly. Here's the straight dope. I've been suspecting something like that. Dirkes and me get along because it's to our advantage to do so. We bought out the small outfits before they could grow and challenge us."

"You bought them out, scared them out, or just plain run them off with a gun," Tony said, trying to keep the bitterness out of his voice.

"I may not have paid top dollar, but I never killed a man to get his land," Wilson said angrily.

"How about Dirkes?"

"I already told you I don't trust Dirkes. He aims to be top dog on this range and at the same time win the respect of the town through Wilma, his wife, and her charities. He's a complicated man. With Felicitas he was hard and bitter, but now he knows respect is important if he wants to enjoy his power."

"His wife is a beautiful and kind woman," Tony said. "How come she married a man like Dirkes?"

"You tell me. Maybe she's ambitious on her own account, or maybe she's hoping for atonement."

"What do you mean by that?"

"It's rumored that she sent the man who loved her to his death, to please Dirkes."

Tony felt a surge of anger and remorse.

"Baudry said Folger was ramrodding the play."

"Don't believe all you hear. Dirkes might want it to look like that to keep his name clean. He's afraid to come out in the open, afraid of losing his wife. After what he put up with Felicitas, Wilma's an angel. She does have her good points; she's using Dirkes' money to do good. Dirkes hates that scrawny boy she adopted, but he can't do anything about it. I hear she's going to adopt a girl, Annie Jeffers. Her paw was killed in a brawl in the Red Garter, and her mother has lost interest in the kid."

"Let's get down to cases, Wilson. Do you want me to play along with Baudry and Fats?"

"For the time being. You might run some cattle across on your own, salt them where Folger won't look. Then I can brace Carl and demand the right to search his range."

"You ain't strong enough for a showdown with Dirkes," Tony said candidly.

"I can get the Cattlemen's Association behind me."

For the next three weeks Tony avoided the town and put in as much time as he could outdoors. He gained twenty pounds that first month, and his skin began to tan and develop wrinkles. Twice he ran into Baudry and Fats easing some cows onto Box-X range, and he gave them a hand. Once, when he was sure nobody saw him, he ran a bunch over on his own.

One night after he had washed the supper dishes, he was surprised to find Kent Wilson in back of the bunkhouse talking to Baudry. Kent, evidently just learning to smoke, was awkwardly rolling a quirly, getting more tobacco on the ground than he did in the paper. When Egan passed them, they stopped talking. He wondered what Kent had in common with Baudry. Probably just growing pains, a boy's ambition to be with men. He remembered what Wilson had said about Kent being impatient to take charge of the ranch. He put the thing out of his mind when he entered the bunkhouse; it was no affair of his.

When the month was up, he asked Wilson to take him out of the kitchen and give him a regular riding job.

"I reckon it's time for a change. You don't look like the same man any more, Brad. You got color in your face, and them clothes are getting a mite too tight for you. Here; I'll give you your month's pay. Being as you rode the range in between kitchen chores, I'm giving you a rider's wages."

"I didn't bargain for that; I bargained for flunky pay," Tony said.

"I owe you more than a rider's wages, boy. When you took to spying for me, you invited a bullet. I'm glad it turned out like it did."

"I won't argue with you, Wilson. Give me fifty dollars out of my money in the safe, too. I aim to go to town and buy me an outfit."

"Keep your eyes peeled for Finney and Folger; they both got a grudge against you, Brad."

"I reckon I can look out for myself."

Saturday, after he finished his morning chores, Tony prepared to go into Sabado. He made sure his gun was cleaned and oiled. As he was leaving the bunkhouse, Abe Jones stopped him.

"I reckon I'se got some stuff to buy in town, Brad. If yo'all don' mind, I'll ride along with you."

Tony smiled, knowing the Negro's real reason for wanting to go with him. "What do you want, Abe? I'll buy it for you."

"I reckon I'll do my own buyin', pardner."

"You're coming to side me in case of trouble. That might just invite trouble, Abe. You and me is sort of paired off now in everybody's mind. I sided you, a favor you'll have to square. Alone, I can take care of myself, but I can't take care of both of us."

Abe frowned and smacked his lips. He ran a hand across his ornamental mustache.

"Yo'all ain't got a high opinion of me, have you? Why you think I can't hold up my end in a fight?"

Tony laughed. "I didn't mean it that way. I'm sorry, Abe. I meant that I can't keep us both out of trouble. An insult I might square with words; you would counter with flying fists."

"I'm strong as a ox, man. Ain't nobody goin' to tangle with me barehanded."

Tony shrugged. "I don't own the town. You can do as you please."

Lucy stopped him as he rode out the lane past-the big house. She had her wild hair brushed into a semblance of order, and she wore a starched blue frock. She had a smile on her round face.

"Seeing as you're riding my horse, you can buy me a yard of red ribbon," she said coquettishly.

Tony knew she had fixed herself up just for him, and it disturbed him. He had no time for the flirting of a girl-child. Her allusion to his gray horse irked him.

Abe caught up with him while he was still pondering the young girl's attitude.

"Reckon I'll ride along with you, suh," Abe said politely.

"I can't keep you from going into town, Abe, but don't go in with me. Furthermore, don't dog me, neither. If theres' a fight in broad daylight, it will have to be more or less fair. That's all I ask."

"Brad Regan, you're mighty techy. I'll be seein' you."

With that Abe kicked his horse and rode on ahead. Egan cantered the gray, letting the distance between them grow. He had no intention of getting into a brawl today. To confirm his resolve, he dismounted and put his gunbelt and gun into one of his saddlebags.

The Holytown section of Sabado was busy with Saturday shoppers. There were grub wagons in from the ranches for supplies. Indians from the reservation, swathed in their colorful blankets, roamed the street. Tony wondered why there were so many people, even a good sprinkling of Mexicans from across the border. Then he saw one of the signs. It was a holiday, a holiday he should have remembered.

It was Fra Quintada day, in memory of the missionary priest who had built the mission on the outskirts of town. He crossed the street to Lupe's Café. He had an account to settle there.

Lupe's Café was full of revelers, and she had two girls helping her to handle the crowd. The counter was full, so Tony found a seat at a table in a corner of the room. He heard a commotion over to one side and, looking in that direction, he was startled to see Blackie Folger, Vern Veldon and a couple of other men busy with their meal. The four men had not seen him come in, but Lupe had.

"*Buenas dios, amigo.* You look more better now, color in the face, bistek on the bones, but you still not have new *pantalones* or *chaparajos.* You wear the same battered sombrero."

"Lupe *amiga*, I came to settle my bill before I spend all my money on clothes," said Tony, grinning.

"What beel?" Lupe pretended not to recall.

"I had two meals here last time I was in town. My week was up a long time ago." Tony laid one of the ten-dollar gold pieces Wilson had given him from the safe. "There. I want more of your bistek, frijoles and tortillas. But no milk—coffee. That ought to cover it." He indicated the gold coin.

"Too much. Give me wan seelver peso."

"I'm adding a tip for service. Lupe, I love you; swallow your pride and take the money. I'll bet you've fed many a hungry cowboy here without pay."

Lupe put her hands on her hips and shook her head. "I take the dinero, but only to save for you. By morning you be busto."

Tony watched Lupe walk away with her proud swinging gait, and as he followed her across the room with his eyes, he saw one of the men at Folger's table reach across and nudge Folger. Folger turned his dark, lean face, and his black eyes pinched almost shut. Tony stared back with no expression on his face. When Folger turned around, there was a new stiff set to his wide shoulders.

Tony meant to bend over backwards to avoid trouble, and he wondered if Baudry had spoken to Folger about how he, Brad Regan, had agreed to go in with the rustling bit. He saw Lupe coming back with his platter of food, and as she passed Folger, he stood up, barring her way.

Taking the platter from her before she could object, Folger said, "You sure are rushed here today, Lupe honey. Reckon I'll give you a hand with the customers."

Folger turned and approached Tony, who was facing him at the far side of the table. Just before he reached the table, Folger pretended to trip. He lunged forward, dropping the platter of hot food into Tony's lap. Tony leaped up, brushing the food to the floor and holding onto his temper for all he was worth.

"Oops, sorry, sodbuster!" Folger said, grinning.

Lupe, infuriated, jumped on Folger's back, pounding him with her fists. "You peeg! Why for you do thees? You get out my place, Blackie! You go eat weeth the dogs!"

"Wait a minute—wait a minute!" Blackie said, trying to shake her loose. "It was an accident, Lupe honey!"

"I'm no your honey! You get a broom; you sweep up thees floor!"

"I'll pay for the food!" Blackie offered, still trying to defend himself.

Tony, stiff as a board, stood by the table, bits of food sticking to his clothes. He gave Folger a look that left no questions as to the emotions behind it. He spoke in a soft, controlled voice.

"Never mind, Lupe. Let the gentleman go. I'll pay for the dinner, and I'll sweep up the floor."

Folger, taken aback, momentarily ogled Tony. Then a sneer twisted his face, and he said with ill-concealed rancor, "Thank you, pilgrim. You sure are a generous man." He followed the remark with a loud guffaw of laughter. Going back to his table, he threw some money down and motioned his companions to follow him outside.

With the eyes of the other diners on him, Tony brushed himself off, then proceeded to pick up the platter and scoop the food off the floor.

"One of the *muchachas* weel clean up the floor, Brad Regan. Why you no punch his face in?"

"Lupe, I wouldn't want to repay your kindness by helping to wreck your café. Blackie Folger is scared, and he's trying to prove to himself that he's not. I think I've got him buffaloed. He don't understand me, but one thing he knows in his rotten soul is that I'm not scared of him."

Lupe brought him another dinner, and after eating it, he went outside and across the street to the general store. There he bought a complete new outfit of clothes. He bought extra flannel shirts and sox and underwear. In the back room of the store, he donned California pants, a flannel shirt, new stitched boots, and a fawn-colored sombrero with a rawhide band. He pulled on the batwing chaps and looked at himself in the cracked mirror. He couldn't suppress a grin. He didn't know if he looked better or worse than he did in his bib and tucker. The new outfit reminded him of a tenderfoot trying to play cowboy. He shrugged. The chaps would soon get warped, the boots scuffed and the hat curled around the brim.

Going back through the store, he passed the ribbon counter and remembered Lucy Wilson's request. With a sheepish grin, he bought a yard of red ribbon and, when it was rolled and wrapped, shoved it into the breast pocket of his flannel shirt. Picking up his other bundles, he headed for the street. Because his arms were full, a customer opened the door for him. His vision impaired by the bundles in front of him, he stepped out on the porch, which was a couple of steps higher than the boardwalk.

He was not aware of Blackie Folger and his cronies until he heard his loud laugh and raucous voice.

"Well, look at this brand-new cowboy!"

Before Tony had a chance to brace himself, Blackie put out his foot and tripped him. With his arms full, Tony had no way to catch himself. He plummeted down the steps and landed on his face in the dust of the street. Even above the humiliation and the shock, he felt an overwhelming fury. He lay there for a moment with his bundles strewn about him. Even the package of ribbon had slipped from his breast pocket. A big gust of laughter greeted his discomfiture as he lay there, trembling with anger. A man picked up one bundle that had broken open and held up his underwear for all to see.

"Now ain't that pretty!" he crowed.

The people in the street stopped to stare at the demonstration, some of them joining in the ribbing and the laughter. Folger found the package of ribbon, which had been torn in the downward plunge.

"Now ain't that something—a shiny red ribbon!"

Tony saw his new hat lying in the gutter. He rose slowly without looking around and retrieved his hat. He dusted it off on the sleeve of his shirt.

"Too bad about your elegant hat, calfboy," Veldon said without smiling.

Tony carefully put his hat on his head and pulled up his pants. Then, swift as a snake he turned full circle and smashed a fist into Folger's face with such force that Folger was knocked flat. Folger, shaking his head in bewilderment, forced himself to a sitting position. Then his eyes cleared and a venomous hate screened them. He snatched for his gun.

Somebody shouted, "The kid's unarmed, Blackie!"

Folger threw his gun aside, and a leer split his face. "That's fine! That's just fine!"

Tony didn't underestimate his position. The weight he had put on during the past month of riding was an asset, but reflexes and judgment had not been sharpened by prison routine. There was no backing down, no more dodging the issue. He might get licked, but Blackie Folger would not go unmarked. Blackie rose cautiously and, when he had his feet under him, lunged in swinging. Tony twisted away from that first onslaught. Blackie hoped to end the fight with one wild charge, but he found his target an elusive one. Tony took the first wild blows on his arm and shoulder; then, twisting around, he cut Folger's face with a glancing blow.

Folger came back snarling, his head down. A hush had come over the crowd at the sight of blood on the dark man's face. Tony waited until Folger was ready to ram him with his head; then he brought up his fist from the knee, an uppercut that smashed Folger's nose. Damaging as the blow was, it didn't stop Folger. Tony felt hard fists batter his stomach and his ribs, and the breath was knocked from him.

Folger's nose was bleeding now, and the taste of blood suffused him with animal cunning. He stopped his wild rushes and stood off, using his superior reach to jab and bruise Tony's face. Tony felt his breath wheezing through his throat, and he brushed aside the jabs in desperation. He got in close once more and sent three swift blows to Folger's bleeding face. One blow opened the cut on his cheek wider, and another increased the damage to his nose. Folger lifted a boot and shoved him back. Tony felt the burning pain in his groin. He shook his head and winced as Folger continued his jabs. Tony felt one eye swelling.

Knowing that if he were blinded he would be cut to ribbons, Tony again got inside of Folger's guard and drove a fist wrist-deep into his guts and another fist to his heart. Folger sat down suddenly, gasping for breath. Tony stood waiting until Folger crawled to his feet. Folger's face was a bloody mask now, and he came in like a frenzied animal. Tony couldn't dodge all of the blows. He felt his head rocked and bruised, but his new skin was taking the punishment without peeling off. The street was reeling about him, but Tony forced himself to stand. He threw a jab at Folger's bloody nose and backed off. Then he felt a boot hit his ankles, and he fell to the ground.

Abe Jones' voice rose above the hubbub. "Yo'all aim to play dirty, man, I'm gittin' into this ruckus mahself!"

Abe started for the stolid form of Veldon, who had tripped Tony. Before Abe could reach Veldon, a pistol came down on the back of his head, knocking him unconscious. There was a low roar of protest from the crowd. Tony pushed himself up, his one eye closed. He looked for the swaying figure of Blackie Folger and headed for it with all the fury of a wronged man. He swung for Folger's face, wild but telling blows. Folger tried to fight back, tried to get his long arms about Tony's chest. Tony used his own boot then, driving into Folger's thigh and spinning him half around. Folger stood swaying like an aspen in the wind. He turned blindly and staggered away like a blinded, drunken man, not looking at anybody, not seeing anybody.

Tony, himself half blind, staggered about looking for

Folger. Then the last dregs of his energy were gone. He slumped unconscious to the ground. There was a murmur of dismay in the crowd at the sight of two men beating each other insensible, neither willing to give ground. There was a rustling in the ring of bystanders. Ruby Miller forced herself to the side of Tony Egan, her red hair a flaming banner and her flashing brown eyes a warning against interference.

"Carry him into my place," she said in a voice that drew no protest, even from Vern Veldon.

CHAPTER SIX

Ruby had the two men lay Tony on the couch in her sitting room, and then she dismissed them. She got some warm water and gently washed the blood off his face. She noticed with some surprise that his skin had tanned some since she had last seen it, and character lines were faintly etching themselves in his face. As she washed the blood out of his hair, she noticed the scars left by knife and needle. She frowned; she had never seen such scars before.

Abe, who had recovered from the rap on the head, poked his head in the open door.

"I picked up his belonings, ma'am. Tell him I'm taking his horse to the livery barn. Wheah shall I put his purchases, ma'am?"

"Thank you, Abe. Put them on the counter in the store."

"Tell him not to worry, ma'am. Tell him I'll take care of mattahs."

Ruby gave him a sharp look. "Don't get into any trouble over this, Abe. He fought Blackie Folger to a standstill. That should quiet things for a spell."

After Abe left, Ruby turned back to her messy task and studied the face of the man she ministered to. She had seen a mouth like that before, but the nose was different, not so straight. This young, headstrong boy, be he sodbuster or not, reminded her of another time; another time that had ended in disaster and despair. The despair was still eating at her soul like a worm in a rotten apple. If Wilma Logan had not interfered that day, Patch Roger might still be alive, and she would not be trapped within these four walls, unable to extricate herself.

Vern Veldon had waited the proper length of time before he moved in, but she had preferred others, nearer her own age. She had gone with two of them. But one had been beaten up and run out of town; the other had been goaded into an uneven gunfight and killed. She could stand such things no longer, and she had refused to run. Vern had presented himself as a gentleman, but she knew that under the blond hair on his square head lurked the will and determination to prevent others from showing her attention.

Vern had taken a leaf from Dirkes' book, hoping to present a front of respectability while secretly plying his nefarious projects. More to impress Wilma than to please herself, she allowed Veldon to squire her the few times she went anywhere. Again she studied the face she had cleansed and salved, and again memory stirred in her brain.

Tony came out of oblivion slowly. He saw a beautiful face close to his, a crown of red hair and soft brown eyes. He had seen that face often in his dreams, coupled with Wilma's.

"Carrots, Carrots," he mumbled, "what are you doing here?" He saw comprehension dawn in the brown eyes.

"Tony, Tony Egan," Ruby said, and tears welled into her eyes.

The sound of his real name jarred him to sensibility. He opened his eyes wide and looked up at the love and tenderness in her face.

"How did you know me, Ruby?"

"Nobody ever called me Carrot-top or Carrots except you and Patch. Also, I had a vague clue as I washed your face. What made your humpy nose so straight, and your skin so smooth and clear?"

"Do you remember how Dirkes cut me up and stomped me?"

"I shall never forget it. At the trial, your face was a horribly healed scar. There was little resemblance to what you are now. What miracle happened?"

"Maybe it was a miracle. There was a young doctor at the hospital. He had learned a new technique called plastic surgery. Not caring what happened, I let him experiment on my face. I went through many painful and long operations in which he grafted skin from other parts of my body, parts that had been shielded from sun and wind by my clothes. He grated bone and removed the hump from my nose. Do you understand now, Ruby, how I came back looking like a green kid?"

She put her face against his in wonder. "Yes, yes, I can understand. You don't know what it means to me, Tony, having you back. It's like an act of God."

"Amen," Tony said. "Maybe now you understand how I was able to cow Folger that night in the Red Garter; how I bested Finney and the others in the card game; how I dared to fight Folger in the street just now. Folger knows that I'm not what I appear to be, but he doesn't know why."

"Now I know why you asked for Wilma that first day. I'm sorry, Tony."

"You sounded bitter when you called her the best kept woman in town."

"I am bitter, bitter against deceit, ambition, disloyalty. What happened that day shook her up pretty badly. When Felicitas was killed, she married Carl Dirkes, the man who had caused the horrible tragedy involving you and Patch. Her whole sense of values changed, as though she meant to get even with the world."

"You haven't changed, Carrots. Next to Wilma, I thought more of you than any girl I had ever known. But everyone has her breaking point. I saw you go to church with Vern Veldon."

Her face flushed. "I'm glad you came back, Tony. Now I can hold out against him."

"I reckon I'll have to ask you one favor right now."

"Name it, Tony. Now that you're here, I feel safe and strong."

"Keep my identity a secret. I'm still Brad Regan. Get that?"

"Yes, yes, I get it. There's no law that says I can't be nice to a lonesome cowboy, though."

"None but Vern Veldon's law, and I welcome that. Will you go to church with me in the morning?"

"For your sake, no."

"Reckon I shouldn't have asked you that, with my face all cut up and a black eye."

"It isn't that, Tony. You've just taken one beating."

"Vern won't touch me."

"No, Vern won't, but one of his gang will. Get your strength back first."

"I'll be right as rain in the morning."

He got up now to work the stiffness out of his bruises. Ruby followed him out into the shop, where his purchases, tied as neatly as Abe Jones could tie them in torn paper, lay on the counter. The red ribbon was neatly folded beside them.

"Reckon I'll get these out of your way," he said as two women came into the shop.

"A red ribbon," Ruby said, smiling. "Do you have

another girl already?"

"Reckon so. You know her."

"I do?"

"Lucy Wilson. The little brat's trying to throw a hook into me. She claims the horse I brought and paid for. The ribbon is to humor her."

"It's dangerous to humor a woman. To—Brad," Ruby caught herself, "when are you going to humor me?"

"Name it."

"Don't go to Honkytown tonight."

"You're humored," he said shortly. Picking up his bundles, he turned to go.

"You can't take your girl that dirty ribbon. Here, take her this." She cut a wide red ribbon off a bolt on the counter.

"Lucy and me are both grateful, ma'am," he said as he went out the door, ignoring the stares of the two customers.

Abe met him outside with their horses, and tied some of the bundles on the back of his saddle. Brad put the neatly folded ribbon in his pocket.

On reaching the Wilson ranch, Tony dismounted and went to the door of the big house. He was glad it was Lucy who answered the door.

"Here's your red ribbon, button. Wear it in good health."

"Here's your kiss, cowboy," she said, and before Tony could dodge she tiptoed and kissed him on his mouth.

"That payment was wasted," he said, catching his breath. "The ribbon is a gift from Ruby Miller."

Lucy frowned. "What were you doing with Vern Veldon's woman?"

"She's not Vern Veldon's *woman*," Tony said grimly. "Let's say she's his friend. When you're older, Lucy, you'll know the difference."

He turned and walked away.

"You look more like a cowboy with your new clothes, honey," she called after him. "Likewise, I know more than you think I do !"

Tony didn't look back. The bunkhouse was deserted, as all the men had gone to Honkytown for their Saturday fun. Tony put his purchases away on the shelf over his bunk. Then he went to the cook shack.

"Hello," Chow Lee greeted him. "You been fightee?"

"I fell in a meat grinder, Chow Lee. Give me a steak."

"I cookee right now chop chop."

"Raw. For my eye."

"Me give gow yuk for eye, fie yuk, steak for stomach."

Chow Lee put the food on the stove and proceeded to tie a piece of raw beef over his eye. Tony ate the steak and potatoes and a big bowl of Chow Lee's rice pudding with custard. Abe came in and helped himself to soup and beef stew that was hot on the back of the stove. Later Tony and Abe played poker in the bunkhouse, Tony teaching him the finer points of the game, and

Abe telling Tony how he had happened to come West. He had been with a wagon train of destitute Southerners who were massacred by Indians.

"The colah of mah skin saved me, Brad. Them redskins figured I was somethin' special, lak a black sheep in a herd. I threatened them with voodoo, and they was glad to get rid of me." He laughed.

Before he went to sleep, Tony vowed that he would get up early and go to church in the morning. He meant to set a precedent so that the next Sunday, when he squired Ruby Miller to church in defiance of Vern Veldon, people would know him as a church man.

He left at daylight for the two-hour ride into town and arrived there just as the people were gathering for the service. From a distance he watched them go in, Dirkes in broadcloth and white linen, Wilma in a flowered dress and plumed hat. His heart hurt at the sight of her, but the hurt turned into anger as he saw Vern Veldon proudly leading Ruby Miller up to the door. Tony moved to go in with the stragglers. He had no Sunday clothes yet, but he was dressed in new flannel and denim. Entering the room which hummed with low voices, Tony took a seat at the rear. He turned his head and looked at Wilma seated regally at the new organ. She caught his eye and beckoned to him. He rose, curious, and went to the platform.

"I heard you had another scrape, Brad," she said in a low voice.

"Unavoidable."

"You seem dogged by bad fortune, yet you always come out on top. Even the flunky job must be good for you; you look like a new man."

"If you called me up here to discuss my fortune, I'll sit down, ma'am."

"You know my name; use it."

"Yes, Mrs. Dirkes."

People, including Carl Dirkes, heard them talking and turned their heads. Dirkes' hard, flat face was a thundercloud. He did not relish his wife taking up with a sodbuster turned cowboy.

"Be stubborn if you must. I want you to sing a solo just before the sermon. I usually play the organ then while the people pray."

Tony was taken aback.

"I ain't a church singer, ma'am. Honkytown is my style."

"Your voice is plaintive and appealing; it might shake some of these hidebound hypocrites up a little."

Dirkes had turned his head again, and the look on his face gave Tony an idea. Dirkes was jealous. It was hurting him to have his wife talk to a drifter. All right; he would hurt him some more.

"I know 'Rock of Ages,' "he said off hand. "Reckon, though, I'd be better pumping the bellows stick."

"I prefer to have you sing. Sit on the end of the bench until I give you the word." She called to the boy behind the organ, "All right, Bennie; start pumping."

The organ music welled forth, filling the small church with pulsing sound. The Reverend Spreck had his own routine for the services, which opened with a prayer.

After the prayer the congregation stood and sang a hymn to which Wilma played the accompaniment. Tony sang along with them to warm up his voice.

The time for his solo came while the minister was saying a silent prayer before the sermon. He stood behind Wilma so he could read the words in the hymnal on the organ.

"Rock of ages, cleft for me—"

The words were a plaintive voice in the silence, begging the mercy of the Lord. When he came to the last line, he saw Wilma stiffen, and her shoulders shook as though in a stifled sob.

"Save from guilt and make me pure."

Ruby turned her head deliberately and gave him a strange, sympathetic look. He sat down without looking at Wilma.

When the meeting broke up, Carl lost no time in coming to claim her.

"Just a minute," Wilma said when he reached a ham-like hand for her soft arm. She turned to Tony. "Won't you come and sing at the Sabado Queen next Saturday, Brad? I promised not to cut in."

"We don't need no cowboy singer at the Sabado Queen," Carl cut in. "Who the devil are you, younker?

You been stirring up trouble ever since you been here. My advice is for you to travel on."

"I'll think it over, sir," Tony said politely, but inside he was seething.

"And stay away from my woman, understand? You got the people talking already. I have no intention of being deceived by a raw kid from nowhere."

Wilma gave Carl a scathing look. "Do you mean to stand here and insult your wife in front of everybody? You're accusing me of loose conduct because I befriended a stranger. Are you that unsure of yourself, Carl?"

Carl's face turned beet red. His big hand closed on her arm and propelled her outside. Tony hung back. As Ruby went out the door with Veldon, she turned and gave Tony a signal. He waited until the people had dispersed before emerging from the church. He mounted his horse and rode down to Lupe's Café. He had not eaten breakfast yet, and he was hungry.

"You crazy, loco keed. Don't you have trouble enough yesterday? I see them carry you to Ruby Miller. *Señor* Veldon he see them, too. I hear him tell another hombre, 'That loco sodbuster has got to be taken care of.' You make everywan worry."

"Lupe, get me a stack of hot cakes, a slab of ham, a pot of coffee, and don't worry about me." He grinned.

Other late risers straggled in after their strenuous celebration of the night before. Fats and Baudry were among them. They stopped near his stool.

"I don't think you got it right the other day, Brad," Baudry said. "Beating Folger up wasn't exactly what I meant when I asked if you were *in*."

"He asked for it, and I obliged him. I didn't get off easy myself."

"A draw with Folger ain't nothin' to be ashamed of."

"Does he know I'm in on the deal?"

"What makes you ask that?"

"If he knew I was in on the deal, he wouldn't have picked a fight with me. I don't believe you even told him about me."

"Fact is, I was waiting to see how you proved out."

"Have I proved out?"

"So far, one hundred percent."

"Then tell him. If you don't, it might come to killing next time we meet."

"I'll tell him. I wouldn't want to see you dead."

Fats and Baudry moved on. Tony finished his hot cakes and asked Lupe if he could go out the back way through the kitchen.

"*Seguro, amigo*. Why for?"

"I want to see Ruby without being spied on by Veldon or one of his friends."

"You always look for trouble. Why?"

"Lupe, a man has got to tackle trouble when it's born; otherwise it grows too big for him."

"I theenk you *poco loco*."

In the alley, Tony walked the few steps to the rear

of Ruby's shop. She had definitely signaled him as she had left the church, and he meant to find out what the signal meant. He found a door and knocked on it. He waited a moment and then knocked again. This time he heard someone stirring inside. Soon the door opened and Ruby stood there, beautiful in her Sunday frock with pearl earrings lying against the soft redness of her hair. He remembered the little freckles across the bridge of her pert nose.

"Come in quickly," she said, pulling his arm. She shut the door.

"Are you alone?" Tony asked, curious.

"Vern just left."

"You signaled me as you left the church; right?"

"Yes. I enjoyed your song. Wilma used you as a pawn to make Carl squirm. She enjoys hurting people. It's as though she had a grudge against the world and enjoyed seeing people humiliated."

"Aren't you a mite hard on her, Carrots? She has adopted a boy who needs love and care. She is adopting a girl. That night when she nursed me in her room at the Sabado Queen, she was kind. She even even apologized for horning in on my singing."

"I'll withhold judgment," Ruby said shortly. "I didn't call you here to talk about Wilma. On the way to church, Vern told me he was going to be away for a while. I thought you might like to know."

"Where is he going?"

"He never tells me. He does this every once in a while. He comes back feeling smug and tries to spend money on me, but I refuse."

A vague idea took shape in Tony's mind. He recalled the item he had read in the newspaper while waiting for his shave in the barbershop. The Las Cruces stage had been held up and robbed of a shipment of gold. He mentioned the item to Ruby.

"Did Veldon take off about that time?" he added.

She thought a moment. "Come to think of it, he did. Why?"

"A hunch I've got."

He remembered the book in the bottom drawer of Wilma's dressing table that he had looked through when recovering his money. There were dates and amounts, accounts of murders and robberies. The first date had been his own day of reckoning, and the last entry had been very recent. It could have been the gold taken in the Las Cruces stage robbery.

When Tony left Ruby, he rode to the stage station and found the agent there awaiting the Sunday stage from Prescott.

"I'm Brad Regan," he told the agent. "I wondered if you could give me a piece of information."

"You might try me, son."

"How often is gold shipped from Las Cruces?"

The agent looked at him suspiciously. "Why? You aimin' to hold up the stage?"

Tony grinned. "Not likely. When is the next shipment due to pass through?"

"That's secret information, boy. Even I ain't told about it."

"Some secrets have a way of slipping out. I read in the paper that the stage was robbed last month."

"You're a mite nosy, ain't you?"

"I was just curious."

"You a bounty hunter?"

"Could be," Tony replied. It was not a complete lie; he and Patch had practiced the trade until the girls had talked them out of such a dangerous and unappreciated calling.

"Can't help you, lad. I wouldn't advertise my status if I was you. A bounty hunter ain't real popular around here, specilly not down in Honkytown."

"I just thought I'd ask. Thanks for nothing."

He rode on out to the ranch, his brain spinning. When he reached the ranch, Abe was lying on his bunk reading a Bible.

"How did the Lohd's day turn out for yo', pahdner?" Abe inquired.

"Eventful. I even sang a solo in church."

"Will the Lohd's wonders never cease?" commented Abe.

"Nobody left the church," Tony bragged a little. "I've got a favor to ask you, Abe."

"Ah'm yoah man, Brad. Name yoah trouble."

"I got a hunch there's going to be a stage robbery somewhere between Las Cruces and Vanishing Mountain. We could be in on it."

"Yoah mean us'n gwine rob the stage?"

"Not exactly."

"What yo'all mean not 'zactly?"

"We're going to rob the robbers."

"You crazy man. How we all gwine do that?"

"I've had experience. I'll leave a note at the house so Wilson will know we've not run away completely."

CHAPTER SEVEN

Tony and Abe rode under the stars toward Vanishing Mountain, so named because a man could lose himself there without leaving a trace. The shale ridges, the streams, dry washes could swallow up a trail.

"Do you know this country well, Abe?" Tony asked.

"I'm not too familiar with the land heah, Brad. I only been around heah foh the past three yeahs. Reckon I got a good nose for directions, though."

"I figure the stage will be held up about twenty miles this side of Las Cruces. There's a grade there leading up to the pass on the other side of the mountain. There's plenty of scrub growth there and piñon trees for the robbers to hide in until the stage comes along. They take the booty and then vanish into the mountains."

"Foh a man who jest drifted into Sabado, you seem to know plenty about the country hereabouts."

"I've been over the Las Cruces grade before, Abe."

"I ain't never done no hijackin' before, Brad. Reckon I know a few Indian tricks, though."

"It won't be too dangerous. We pull these socks over

our heads so we can see through the holes we cut in them. You keep your gloves on so they can't see the color of your hands. You don't have to say anything; I'll do the talking and give the orders."

"Yo'all talk mighty cool, man. How we gonna catch them fellahs?"

"Just leave it to me, Abe. You're not scared, are you?"

"Man, I ain't 'zactly anxious foh the job, but I ain't scahed, neither. Stage robbahs ain't noted foh their civility, an' they usually packs guns."

"We're packing guns, pardner," Tony reminded him. "If it will make you feel better, I was a bounty hunter once."

"Yo' was a which?"

"Bounty hunter." He looked in Abe's direction but in the semi-darkness he couldn't tell what was in the black mans' eyes.

"That's a dirty word in some places," Abe said thoughtfully.

"I never killed a man for the reward. Me and my pardner, Patch Roger, we brought them in alive, and they stood trial."

"An' yo'all collected the reward; right?"

"That was our pay-off. We were really free-lance lawmen, saving the sheriffs a lot of riding and hunting and ridding the country of no-good shunks. We didn't see no harm in it. I don't now."

"Is that what we's doin' now, Brad? We goin' to git

us some bounty?"

"Not directly."

"If we steal the gold from the stealers, we cain't keep it 'thout we be robbahs, too."

"I've got a plan that will leave us smelling like a rose, Abe."

"Roses also got thohns on 'em, Brad."

"Only the careless get stuck. When we throw down on them fellows, we got to be careful to use no names."

"Suppose they staht shootin'? What then?"

"I'll take care of that," Tony said grimly.

When they reached the east side of Vanishing Mountain, Tony avoided the used trails and led the way through the chaparral and junipers higher up above the pass. Reaching a spot above at the halfway marker on the grade, Tony tensed. Far below, near the stage road, he saw the blinking of a small fire. The men he was trailing were more obliging than he had hoped for, giving him their location.

"You might light and take a nap if you want, Abe."

"That fahr down yonder mean something?"

"I reckon."

"If we go to sleep now, we won't wake up until noon."

"You sleep. I'll keep watch. I'm used to staying up two nights in a row sometimes."

Abe stretched out on the ground without blanket or saddle for a pillow. Tony sat and listened to the night sounds and savored the acrid scent of chaparral and juniper. An owl hooted making Tony uneasy. He heard the distant wail of a coyote like a soul in travail, ending the weird moan with a series of sharp barks. . . .

The morning dawned reluctantly, with the scent of pine and mesquite on its cool, fresh breath. He looked uneasily down the side of the mountain and made out the dark forms of the men still sleeping beside the dead ashes of the fire they had built the night before. They must feel safe and concealed in their hide-out, little dreaming that his eyes were on them. The stage should be leaving Las Cruces about now, and with the fresh horses it should pass there within the hour.

"Wake up, Abe," he said in a guarded voice, nudging the Negro with the toe of his boot. Abe, like most outdoor men, was alert in an instant.

"Is the stage comin'?" he asked, rising and brushing himself off.

"Not yet. Are you hungry?"

"I reckon I'll leave off the vittles ontil this caper is over."

"Suit yourself. There's some hardtack and jerky in my saddlebag."

"Thank you kindly, Brad. I'll wait to eat till my stomach ain't jittery."

"We've got to get down near the road without being seen. We can follow that ravine yonder, and that should bring us out near the road a little way up from where the stage robbers are waiting."

"Ouah hosses is gwine to git plumb starved an' thusty, Brad."

"I know a place where we can rest up and graze the horses once the caper is over."

"Them men gwine chase us."

"I know all the fugitive tricks ever invented, Abe."

When they reached a jutting point of rock near the road, Tony halted. He turned to Abe Jones.

"All right; pull your stocking on, and be sure none of your skin shows. Keep your gloves on, and have your gun ready. I reckon it won't be too long now."

The sun had come up, and it took the chill off the morning air.

"We keep out of sight until the robbers get the gold and the stage has gone past us. The robbers will head up the road toward the pass before turning off to get lost around Vanishing Mountain. By the time they reach here, they should have their masks off so we can make out who they are."

"If we identify them, they gotta kill us, Brad," Abe warned.

"They won't know who we are if we keep our masks on. Unless they catch us red-handed before we give them the slip, we can ride back to Sabado as safe as a babe in a cradle."

"I shoah hopes the good Lowd is on ouah side, pardner."

"Hold my horse, Abe," Tony said, and he climbed up the rock so he could see down-trail. From his vantage point he could see a banner of dust far off, heralding the approach of the stage. He saw no sign of the four bandits, but that was to be expected. He called down to Abe:

"The stage is coming!"

"Sho' nuff," Abe replied.

The holdup took place like a well rehearsed stage play. Two men sprang into the road from either side, their faces masked with bandanas. The driver pulled the horses to a stop, and the man riding shotgun threw his hands in the air. The passenger compartment was not even molested. Tony saw the men shouting, but he couldn't hear what was said. The shotgun slid a small box off from behind the seat, and it fell to the ground. The guard and the driver were forced to throw their guns down, and then the stage proceeded on its way.

Tony and Abe were hidden from the road by the out-cropping of rock, and Tony lay where he was to watch the proceedings. The robbers threw the guns from the stage crew into the brush at one side of the road; Tony suspected the driver and guard would pick them up on their way back. The robbers then pried the box open and took out what looked like small loaves of bread, but Tony knew they were gold bars. A fifty-pound gold bar wouldn't be very big, but it would be worth ten or twelve thousand dollars. One of the men, on a pinto horse, put one of the bars in each of his saddlebags to balance the load. They had already pulled down their masks, and now they mounted and started riding up the grade.

Tony scrambled down off the rock.

"Be sure your sock mask is in place, Abe. One look

at your skin, and they'll know for sure it's you."

"Reckon mah skin is a sickly green this minute."

"Get mounted," Tony ordered.

They rode the few feet to where the road skirted the outcropping. The sounds of the robbers' voices could be heard as they joked and laughed among themselves. As they came into view, Tony spurred his horse forward, his rifle steady in his hand. Abe sided him, holding his six-gun at the ready.

"Stop where you are!" Tony called loud and clear.

"What the devil's going on here?" Folger said.

Unmasked, the four men were helpless to hide their identities.

"I'm not stopping!" Vern Veldon cried, bending over his horse as he started to make a break for it.

Without hesitation, Tony creased Vern's horse's spine at the arch of its neck. The horse dropped unconscious as if poleaxed. Vern was thrown free but lay there dazed for a moment. The other men sat as if stunned. Folger made a move for his gun.

"Don't do it, Blackie," Tony said in a disguised, guttural voice.

Folger stopped his movement, his eyes wavering. He knew the chance he had against a leveled rifle. One of the other men swung his horse around.

"No two-bit sidewinder is scarin' me out!"

The man went for his gun, but before he could lift it, Tony deliberately shot him in the shoulder. The man was spun down out of the saddle.

"You shot me, you coyote!" he screamed, sitting in the dust and holding his bleeding shoulder.

"Throw your guns down, all of you."

Convinced this strange man with a sock over his face meant business, the men complied.

"Collect them, L.G., Tony said, using phony initials.

Abe gathered up the guns and tossed them to one side.

"What in blazes do you want? Name your game, stranger," Folger snarled.

"Untie the saddlebags with the gold bars and drop them on the ground," Tony said in a businesslike voice.

The man carrying the gold hesitated, and Tony let off a shot that flicked the brim of his hat. He hesitated no longer but did as he was told.

"Now all of you mount up and take your wounded friend with you. Hurry it up, Veldon. I can kill at a mile with this rifle; that should take you to the top of the grade. Don't even look back until you're out of sight."

Veldon said in a clear, hard voice, "You just bought yourself a hole six feet underground. You'll never get away with this."

"Why not? Are you four thieves going to take me to court?"

"The only court you'll get is a bullet in the back."

"That's about your stripe, you yellow buzzards."

"You know who we are. It's you or us."

"That's fair enough," Tony said. "Get going." He aimed the rifle menacingly.

They moved on out, the four of them, the wounded man clinging unsteadily to the horn of his saddle. When they were out of earshot, Tony spoke to Abe.

"Gather up their guns; we'll have to hide them. Then go down and move the guns that belong to the stage hands. You'll find them alongside the road in the brush."

Tony got down and picked up the saddlebags containing the gold bars. The two bars weighed a hundred pounds, and it took considerable strength to hoist them to the back of his own saddle. When Abe came back from moving the stage hands' guns to another hiding place, the four robbers were out of sight.

"Let's go," Tony said, mounting. "I know of a proper hide-out not far from here."

Tony Egan knew the broken country around Vanishing Mountain like the palm of his hand. Abe rode with him, silent and thoughtful. Finally he spoke.

"Man, you is the coolest operatah I ever did seed. Them weren't no town dudes you jest fronted out theah; they's the toughest outfit in the country."

"And the crookedest," Tony seconded. "They're in with that driver and guard; the job was too simple. They must have a spy at Las Cruce to tip them off when the gold is going through."

"What can they do with gold bahs, Brad? They gotta sell 'em to the mint."

"Or in Mexico. That half-breed Diaz, needs all the gold he can get to keep his revolution going."

"What can that *metizo* pay off with?"

"Stolen cattle, jewelry, a lot of things that can be turned into money. Then there's another angle. Dirkes is behind this; none of the others have enough brains for it. All Dirkes needs is a gold mine."

"But he ain't got a gold mine."

"I'm going to help him get one." Tony grinned.

"Why does he want a gold mine if he's got gold?"

"I think he's caching the gold for the time being. If he owned a mine that proved to have some gold in it, he could put up a stamp mill, mix the stolen gold with muck from the mine, run it through the mill and smelt it out again as though he'd dug it from the ground."

"Lawsy, man, yo'all have a diverse mind, pahdner."

Crossing country that left no track at all, they came to a deep ravine eaten out of the earth by a million flash floods. In the bottom of the deep cleft there were springs and grassy places that flourished between deluges. Tony stopped near a shallow cave and dismounted.

"Here we are. We'll turn the horses loose and let them graze while we gnaw on some of this dry food. Then I'm taking a short nap while you stand guard. When I wake up, I'm heading for Prescott."

"Yo' what?"

"Heading for Prescott with the gold. You're going back to the Tall-W. Don't tell anybody what happened. Nobody knows you were in on the hijack, not even the robbers."

When Tony reached Prescott, he stabled his horse and

got a room at the hotel. He had taken a shorter route than the stagecoach, and he had not stopped for fresh horses and to pick up and discharge passengers. He figured the stage wouldn't be in until nearly evening. His main problem was the gold. He had solved that by burying the saddlebags containing the gold under a big pile of hay where it would be safe for the time being. At the hotel he washed, combed his hair and got a shave at the barbershop. Although he had been in Prescott many times in former years and had been shaved by the same barber, not even the barber recognized him.

Near the time he expected the stage to arrive, he sauntered out into the street across from the district offices of the stage company, which were above the large station that included the telegraph office. When the stage came rocking down the narrow mountain road into Prescott, it required no newspaper to herald its approach. News of the holdup preceded it down the street, and when it stopped at the station it was surrounded by a curious crowd of people. The agent came out into the street, and the driver got down, talking and gesticulating. He opened the stage door to let the passengers alight. A cowboy stepped out, followed by a slim man with a long jaw, wearing town clothes. The man turned to help a lady out, taking her hand with a slight bow. Tony caught a glimpse of the woman, who had corn-tassel hair and violet eyes. A gasp escaped his lips, and he drew back out of sight. The woman was Wilma Dirkes.

Overcoming his surprise, Tony wondered what she was doing in Prescott, and if the man in the town clothes was with her or had just been a chance passenger. She walked with the man, not to the hotel but up the street, and disappeared into the door of some kind of office. This was a complication Tony had not counted on. There could be a dozen reasons for Wilma to be in Prescott: shopping for some of the fine clothes she wore; visiting friends. He had hoped to leave Prescott unidentified.

But Wilma's presence did not change the plan he had in mind. When the crowd about the stage had dispersed, he crossed the street and went into the station. It was a large, barren room with a potbellied stove in the middle of the floor, a freight counter and a ticket window. He accosted the bald-headed agent.

"I'd like to see the district manager of the stage line," he said.

The man looked up, annoyed, his mind still on the robbery. "I'm afraid he's too busy to talk to you. We just had another holdup on the Las Cruces stage. If it keeps up, the insurance companies will refuse to underwrite us."

"Reckon he'll be glad to hear what I've got to say," Tony persisted.

"Who are you?"

"A pilgrim passing through. I saw the holdup."

The agent's face brightened. "You sure about that?"

Tony's voice hardened. "You calling me a liar?"

"No, I'm just upset. Tell me about it."

"I'll tell Mr. Handley, the manager, if you quit wasting time with your questions.

"Go upstairs to the door on the left. His name's on the door."

Upstairs, Tony entered a well-lighted room furnished with a roll-top desk and a half-dozen Wells Fargo chairs. A florid man with worry furrows over his gimlet eyes looked up from the paper he was reading.

"Who are you and what do you want?" Handley asked.

"I'm Brad Regan."

"I haven't got time right now."

"You've got time to hear me, Mr. Handley. I've got your gold."

"You what?" The portly man half rose from his chair. "You rob our stage, and then you've got the gall to come here and brag about it?"

"I didn't rob the stage, and I'm not bragging."

"You just said that you had the gold."

"I robbed the robbers. I saw the holdup, and I robbed the riders."

"You mean to tell me you held up six bandits and politely relieved them of their stolen gold?"

"Who said there were six of them?" Tony smiled slightly, realizing the driver had made up a story to absolve himself.

"The driver and the shotgun."

"What else did they tell you?"

"That they were clubbed on the head by a man who crawled up over the stage from the back. When they came to, the stage was moving up the road, and the gold was gone."

"That's a right nice fairy tale, sir. What did the passengers say?"

"They couldn't see much from inside the coach. They were thankful to be unmolested." Handley shrugged. "What's your story?"

"There were four robbers. I could name them, but I won't."

"You admit having the stolen gold. What's to prevent me from calling the marshal and having you arrested?"

"Common sense. You want the gold back, don't you?"

"How come you're doing the stage company favors?"

"No favor. I'm claiming the ten percent reward money."

"Go ahead and talk."

"You've got a spy on the line who tips off the gang when the gold is going through. I don't know him yet. The driver and the guard seemed a mite too co-operative when they were held up. They made no pretense of resistence."

"If you know so much, name the robbers."

"Not yet. I want you to give me a job."

"What kind of a job—swamper?"

"No, special agent. I think I can stop these robberies for you. This will have to be just between you and me. I'll have to work undercover."

"You walk in here and ask me to give you a job like that? You're loco, man. Why should I trust you?"

"I brought your gold back, didn't I?"

"I haven't seen it yet."

"You will. You pay me a hundred a month and expenses if I stop the robberies, and if I don't stop them, you pay me nothing. I need some official standing, though. One of your agent's badges will do."

Handley was thoughtful. He asked more questions, probed and pondered. Finally he said, "You'll have to sworn in by the marshal as a deputy."

Tony felt sure Jake Eby was still marshal. Jake had been marshal five years before when Tony had been jailed. Jake had been there when he was released from the territorial prison. Jake would know him, and he didn't want to chance that yet. In fact, Jake had helped get his sentence shortened because of good behavior, and because he had volunteered for the experimental surgery.

"You can swear me in yourself; it will suit me. I don't want anybody to know what I'm doing, not even the marshal."

Handley shrugged. "Bring in the gold, and you've got the job."

"It might take me some time to get the goods on the man behind the gang," Tony said. "In the meantime, I must have a free hand."

"We can't lose anything on your offer. If you find yourself boxed in, send me word. Now bring the gold."

Tony went out the back end of the hall, taking the steps that led down to the alley. At the livery barn, he dug out the saddlebags containing the gold bars. He threw the heavy burden across his back and went back through the alley and up the stairs. Nobody paid any attention to him, as many men lugged saddlebags around. In the office, he closed the door and put his load down, panting with the effort. He took out the gold bars one at a time and laid them on Handley's desk. Handley looked at them in disbelief.

"Well, I'll be doggoned!" he exclaimed.

"Can you keep the fact that the gold has been recovered quiet for a while? If the robbers think the hijacker still has the gold, they might tip their hand as to who their leader is."

"How about the reward?" Handley asked. He stared at Tony. "You smell like a bounty hunter to me. No ordinary man could do what you did and live to tell about it. You sure we haven't met before?"

Tony shook his head. He had collected bounty in Prescott, but not directly from the stage company.

"I'll have to have the bounty money now for working capital. If I make good on the job, you pay me back what I spend in addition to my wages."

"Fair enough. But suppose I give you the twenty-five hundred dollars; that would be about ten percent of what the bars are worth. I can't keep an amount like that off the book longer than the end of the month. Then I'll have to report it to the head office. I'm banking money for a lot of people around here, and if they suspect anything crooked—"

"You have the gold bars in your safe; they'll more than guarantee the money."

Handley shrugged and went to the big safe in the corner. He took out twenty-five hundred dollars in bank notes, handed them to Tony and insisted on a receipt. Tony, though he didn't want anything in writing, complied, signing the receipt with the name of Brad Regan. He took the badge Handley offered.

"Let's shake hands on the deal, Handley," Tony said, extending his hand.

Handley put out his chubby hand. "You're taking on a big chore, son. Why you risking all this trouble for the stage line?"

"Let's say it's partly personal with me."

Tony went downstairs, nodded to the agent, and walked into the street.

CHAPTER EIGHT

Wilma Dirkes sat in the carpeted office of Fred Powers, the lawyer with whom she had come to Prescott and whom she knew only by reputation. He had discreetly boarded the stage at Galena, the next stop after leaving Sabado. His answer to her letter had not been very revealing, but he had met her as promised. She knew the danger of the course she was pursuing, but she had made one dreadful mistake in her life, and she did not mean to make another. The drifter, Brad Regan, with his white, smooth, innocent face, had stirred something in her, something she had thought dead. Her beautiful, soft face was a mask of bitterness, and in her large violet eyes lurked shadows of remorse.

Powers, seated at his desk, ran a thin bony hand across his balding head, and his long jaw barely moved when he talked.

"I don't know if you're being very wise, Mrs. Dirkes," he said, his hooded eys studying her.

Wilma felt that he was plucking thoughts from her brain. "I'll be the judge of my wisdom, Mr. Powers."

"But a divorce isn't easy to get, not from a man like Dirkes."

"He's a man like other men, except that he is crooked cruel, and vicious, in spite of the public image he tries to assume."

"That could make it all the more difficult for you," Powers said. "Your accusations would mean nothing in court without proof."

"I have the proof," she said firmly.

"Written proof?"

"I've written it down."

"That wouldn't be much good unless you could find witnesses or evidence of wrongdoing. Even then the divorce would be difficult. You knew what kind of a man he was when you married him, didn't you?"

"I suppose so."

"You couldn't very well divorce him for faults he had when you married him. You might have him tried for his crimes and thrown in jail."

She bit her lip. "That wouldn't be any good. I'd still be married to him."

Powers shrugged his scarecrow shoulders. "You wouldn't have to live with him, though."

"He's too clever to be convicted. How about a Mexican divorce?" she asked in desperation.

He shook his head. "That wouldn't hold here. Even if you got divorced, you'd be penniless. He wouldn't give you anything."

"I would have my self-respect back. I may be able to right a wrong," she said.

"Wrongs can never be righted. Why don't you be sensible?"

"How do you mean?"

"Dirkes is much older than you. He could die, and then you'd have everything," Powers reminded her with a sly expression.

"As the Bible says, 'What does it profit a man to gain the world if he loses his own soul?' You're not suggesting that I kill Carl, are you?"

Powers laughed a cackling laugh. "If he hears you're trying to divorce him, *he* might kill *you*."

She tried to hide the look of panic that came into her eyes. She remembered the circumstances under which Felicitas had died.

"You wouldn't release this information, would you?"

Powers smiled. "Any communication between a lawyer and his client is strictly confidential."

"Besides, the day of my divorce will be the day he goes to jail on the evidence I'll produce in court."

"If you insist on a divorce, I'll give it a try, but I hope you're not underestimating Dirkes." He reached into a drawer and brought out a legal form. In large letters at the top, it read: "Action For Divorce." He shoved it toward her.

"Sign on the bottom line, and I'll fill in the rest later."

Grimly Wilma signed, knowing she might be signing her own death warrant. What she could do once she was divorced, she wasn't sure. She had heard that Tony was out of jail; that was all she knew. She was sure he would go to a place where he was unknown, rather than return to Sabado with his twisted, gruesome features. In some way she might make up to him for the suffering he had been through, was still going through. She stood up, trembling a little at the dangerous step she was contemplating.

"Shall I see you to the hotel?"

"No thank you. I'll go out the back way. I have a friend here I can stay with."

Tony stopped outside the stage office and looked up and down the street, hoping for a sight of Wilma. She was nowhere to be seen, so he walked up the street to the door she had entered with the tall, scarecrow man. He saw on the door the name: "Fred Powers, Attorney At Law." Hesitating a moment to think of an excuse for his invasion, he turned the knob and entered the lavishly furnished and carpeted office.

There was no sign of Wilma, but the hawk-eyed man behind the flat desk looked up at him expectantly. The man was filling out a form at the top of which Tony saw the words. "Action For Divorce." The words meant nothing to him except that some unhappy marriage was about to be dissolved. Divorce was rare and frowned upon, and a divorced woman was an object of curiosity.

"What can I do for you, sir? Powers said.

There was something off-center in the long-jawed face that stared at him, and he could feel the pale eyes picking him to pieces to see if there was a profit to be made.

"I have a mine deal coming up, and I might need a lawyer. I thought I'd stop and get acquainted. My name's Regan—Brad Regan." He extended his hand.

Powers shook hands, and though his grip was firm enough, his bony hand felt clammy.

"I'd be glad to be of service to you," Powers said, turning the divorce petition over so it couldn't be read.

"Have you any references; men you are retained by?" Tony asked bluntly.

Powers frowned, and his eyes clouded. "I have my law degree, Mr. Regan. That should suffice."

"I just thought you might be representing somebody I know. A law degree don't tell much about a lawyer's capability."

"What part of the country you from?" Powers asked.

"Down Sabado way."

"I'm a lawyer for Carl Dirkes; he's kingpin down that way."

"I should think Hicks, in Sabado, would represent Dirkes."

"It pays to retain a lawyer here at the territorial capital. Then there's Wilson of the Tall-W."

"I reckon those two names should be enough of a

recommendation. If the deal comes off, I'll bring in the papers."

Powers pale eyes grew sharp with interest. "Who is on the other end of the deal?"

"Nobody right now, but there will be."

"New strike?" Powers asked with persistence.

"Could call it that, I guess."

"If you need money, I might raise it for you."

"I'll let you know," Tony said, and left.

Next he went to the assay office and confronted the owner.

"Have you got any gold dust I can buy?"

"I got dust. How much?"

"Say about five pounds or a thousand dollars' worth."

"How come you're buyin' dust? Money's easier to spend."

"Playing a little joke on a friend of mine."

"You usin' it for salt? That's dangerous business."

"It's a joke, and besides, it's my business."

"You said right, friend."

The assayer poured gold onto the pan of a balance and sacked up the five pounds of dust. Tony went back to the hotel, anticipating taking Wilma to supper, but she didn't appear. He waited as long as he could before he went in to eat his lonely meal. He consoled himself with the thought that it would be better if she didn't know he had come to Prescott. If his scheme didn't pan out, she might get hurt if she had knowledge of it.

Tony left Prescott early in the morning, realizing that Wilma had not stayed at the hotel, but with friends. He kept to the stage road until he reached Galena; then he took off for the hills to the north. He wondered if Pop Smith still had his Little Glory mine. It had been a promising prospect when he had filed on it ten years before, but the returns had been grudging little pockets of gold deposited a million years before in an underground stream bed.

He reached the cabin in the rock-ribbed hills near sundown, and found Pop Smith at home, cooking a venison stew that smelled mighty delicious after a day of riding. Pop was delighted to see him.

"Turn your hoss into that fenced pasture by the spring with Nellie, my burrow. Then come in and have chow with me. I'll add some water to the stew an' put in some more ingredients. I'm shore danged glad to see you, pilgrim. I ain't talked to nobody but Nellie fer ages. Even she's gittin' tired of listening to me. Where you headed for?"

"Wait until I put my horse away, Pop; then I'll explain something to you," Tony said. "I'll leave my saddlebags here in the house."

When he was back in the snug cabin with the smell of the stew to whet his appetite, Tony sat on a bench near the sheet iron stove and studied Pop a moment before he began his story. Pop, his gray bearded face beaming at the expectation of hearing news of the world outside his little corner, stood stirring the stew. His back was bent from working in small holes and low tunnels.

"I ain't yet heard yore name, pilgrim," Pop said, looking around.

Tony stared at him, a smile on his lips ."You sure you don't know me, Pop?"

"I don't see many folks. If I knowed you, I'd recomember. I don't never fergit a face," Pop said.

"Did you know a kind of wild younker five or six years ago by the name of Tony Egan?"

"Shore did. Fine feller he were, him an' his side-kick Patch. Them devils went bounty huntin' mostly for the fun of it. I heerd Tony shot his partner an' was hung for murder. I don't know what made the kid turn bad. He seemed right nice when he come up here visitin' me."

"Pop, you heard wrong."

"Some drifter told me the story."

"Pop, brace yourself; I'm Tony Egan."

"Yo're funnin' an old man, boy. Tony had a humpy nose, and he was bigger than you."

"I'm Tony Egan, Pop. I was framed for the murder. I was shot and stomped in the face until I had no features left. Carl Dirkes wanted to get rid of me, so he had me tried in a bought court. He wanted my girl and my homestead. He got both, but I didn't hang. For some reason, right at the last minute, he let it go as manslaughter."

Tony went on to tell of his time in the territorial prison, of the plastic surgery, and of his return under an assumed name.

"Son, you tell a likely story, but you don't look like the Tony Egan I knew."

"Remember that time I was in your mine with you, and that dynamite blast went off before I got under-cover?"

"I should remember. Tore a hole in yore side. I carried you to the cabin and bandaged it up."

Tony stood up and moved close to Pop. "Where would the scar be? Point to it."

Pop touched a spot on Tony's side just above the hip bone. Tony upped his shirt, and the purple remains of the scar were still there.

"Well, I'll be doggoned!" Pop exclaimed. "Let's set an' eat this slumgullion while you tell me what you aim to do."

They sat at the pine board table, which was white from a thousand scourings, and Tony ate silently for a moment until the edge was off his appetite. Then he told what had happened to him since coming back to Sabado.

"Nobody knows me, Pop. I want it that way until I get even with Dirkes. I aim to break him and kill him. I need your help, Pop, so I told you who I am. Promise to keep it a secret."

"I promise, son. How come you want my help? I

ain't no gunswift, and I ain't no fist fighter."

"Don't have to be." Tony grinned. "We'll let him hornswaggle himself. I aim to stay here a day or two."

"Wish you could stay forever," Pop said.

"Pop, what would do if you had ten thousand dollars?"

"That ain't likely to happen, son."

"I think it is, Pop."

"I don't share yore optimism, Tony, but if I had that much money, I'd light outa here, buy me a small place with chickens and a cow, an' a pasture of alfalfee fer Nellie, an' take life easy."

Tony pushed his chair back from the table, went to his saddlebags and drew out the sack of gold dust. He opened it and poured some out into Pop's hand.

"That's real gold dust, Pop," Tony said, putting it back in the sack.

"Where did you git it? You pannin' somewhere?"

"Nope. I bought it, Pop. Do you know how to salt a gold mine?"

"I've heered of it."

"How would you do it?"

"In a vein mine, you've got a problem. In gravel, you can just sprinkle it in. I heerd tell once where the sticks of dynamite was salted. Wherever they was set off gold appeared."

"Have you got dynamite?"

"Reckon I got one unopened box left."

"Good; that's the way we'll do it."

The following day Tony carefully opened the box of dynamite. Over one end of each stick they opened the heavy waxed paper, punched a hole in the soft gelatin and fiilled it with gold dust. Then he carefully put the paper back in place. Putting a couple of ounces of gold in each stick, he salted about half the box. He nailed the boards back in place so that it looked as though it had never been opened, and gave Pop the remainder of the dust.

"You take this into Sabado and noise it around that you've struck gold. Say you're aiming to sell out to anybody with enough money to work the claim," Tony explained. "I think you'll have a buyer before too long."

"Then what? I ask ten thousand dollars for the mine?"

"You ask twenty thousand. We split it, ten for me and ten for you. Dirkes owes me that much. He'll come up here to inspect the mine, and you blast out some rock for him. You can wash the muck in a pan and get the dust out. Open this new box of dynamite so he can't suspect anything, and be sure to keep this side up so you will pick out the loaded sticks."

"Suppose Dirkes don't bite?" Pop asked.

"He will. I've already planted the seed with his lawyer in Prescott."

Tony stayed with Pop Smith another day. When he

reached the Tall-W, the men were out on the range. He turned his horse into the corral, surprised not to see Abe Jones around. In the bunkhouse, there was still no sign of Abe. Worried, Tony went up to the big house. Mrs. Wilson met him at the door, her thin face grave as she plucked at her apron with work-worn hands.

"Is Mr. Wilson here, ma'am?" Tony inquired.

"No, he's gone to Sabado. Won't you come in?"

Tony entered the neat parlor, removing his hat as he did so. "Have you seen Abe Jones around?"

"I certainly have. He's in the back room, hovering between life and death."

"Between life and death?" Tony exclaimed. "What happened?"

"Somebody shot him and left him for dead. How he made it to the ranch I'll never know."

Tony felt a sick feeling go through him. It was his fault. He had been the one to plan the hijacking of the gold, and Abe was paying the price for it. Now he was involving Pop Smith in his fight with Dirkes. Would Pop be the next one to suffer? Even Ruby could be in trouble because of him.

"Did he have a doctor?" Tony asked grimly.

"Dr. Deadmer came out here and fixed him up. He was shot through the neck. It must have knocked him out for a time, and then he came to enough to get on his horse. The horse brought him home, barely alive."

"Could I see him?"

"Lucy is in there sitting with him. It's doubtful he'll live. We hope he will come to and tell who shot him."

Tony knew who had shot Abe, and a new fury warmed him. It had to be either Folger or Veldon. One of the other two men would have had to take the one who was wounded into town. That left Folger and Veldon free to look for the hijackers. They must have run across Abe on his way home the day of the robbery and shot him from ambush. Tony followed Mrs. Wilson to the back bedroom, where he found Lucy quietly crocheting a doily in a chair near the window.

"Hello, Brad," she said, jumping up. "You surprised me."

"How's Abe?"

"Breathing."

Tony went to the bed and looked down at the dark, placid face with its hairy upper lip. The white bandages looked whiter against his black skin. Abe was breathing; that was the only sign of life.

"He didn't say a thing about who might have shot him?" Tony asked.

"He didn't," Lucy said, "but Kent, my brother, heard Baudry and Fats talking in the bunkhouse. They said the stage was held up and that Folger shot one of the robbers, but the other one got away with the gold."

"They called Abe one of the robbers?"

"He's shot, isn't he? Where have you been, Brad?

You and Abe left the ranch the same night," Lucy said suspiciously.

"I'm not one of the robbers, Lucy," Tony replied somberly.

"Somebody might claim you are."

"They couldn't prove it."

"If they killed you, they wouldn't have to prove it," she retorted quickly. "I found the note you left for Dad the night you rode out. It just said you would be back in a day or two. If I testified to that, what alibi would you have?"

"None," Tony said glumly.

"You'd better be nice to me," Lucy warned.

"I don't want you to lie for me, Lucy," Tony said impatiently.

He left the house, after thanking Mrs. Wilson for taking Abe into her home and nursing him. He had come directly to the Tall-W from Galena, avoiding Sabado. Now he had to go to town and find out what was going on.

In town, he went first to Ruby's place, tying his horse to the hitchrail in front of Lupe's Café. There was no one in the shop when Tony entered, but, summoned by the tinkle bell attached to the door, Ruby appeared from her living quarters. Her hand flew to her breast in a gesture more of fright than of surprise when she saw who was there. Her face was grave, and in her brown eyes there was a strange look of warning.

"Hello, Ruby," he said, extending his hands.

"What are you doing here, T—Brad?" she said, almost speaking his true name in her perturbation.

"What the matter? Am I off-range here?"

She put a finger to her red lips as a caution to silence. "I'm very busy, sir," she said, raising her voice.

Sir? The formality irked him. "I want to talk to you, Ruby. Not here where we might be interrupted. Let's go into your parlor." He headed for her living quarters, but she barred the way.

His curiosity and his concern were now fully aroused.

She shook her head until her red hair covered her pearl earrings. "Not now, please. Go away."

He said with a touch of coolness, "Are you entertaining someone back there, madam?"

The *madam* did it. She raised her hand and slapped his mouth. The blow was so unexpected it staggered him. He had forgotten that red hair and temper went together.

"I didn't mean that the way it sounded, Carrots," he said, rubbing the back of his hand across his lips.

"I'm sorry, Brad."

He pushed her aside forcibly, and as he did so he saw the tears in her eyes. A crazy, protective impulse came over him. His arms, that had been pushing her aside, slipped around her shoulders, and he was kissing the tears from her eyes; his mouth closed on hers, and a depth of feeling he hadn't known existed swept over him. She went limp against him, not resisting but complying. He kissed her again, but more gently. Then her lips whispered into his ear:

"Vern Veldon's in there."

Tony, even though he half suspected the truth, felt anger like acid burn in his throat.

"I'm not avoiding him," Tony whispered back. "He's got to know where I stand and where he stands as far as you are concerned, honey."

"He has a broken arm; it's in a sling."

"A broken arm? How did he break it?"

"He said his horse fell with him."

Tony recalled the scene on the road during the hijacking. Veldon's horse had fallen with him, all right. Tony had not suspected that Veldon's arm had been broken. If one robber had taken the wounded man into the doctor, and if Veldon's arm was broken, that left only Folger to have shot Abe Jones. Folger would pay later. Right now it was Veldon's turn.

Tony let go of Ruby, seeing the wonder in her eyes.

"Don't get between us," he warned her as he turned the knob and threw the door open.

CHAPTER NINE

In the back room of the Sabado Bar, Carl Dirkes sat across from the lean, cadaverous figure of Fred Powers. There was no hint of feeling or interest on Carls' flat face as he listened to what Powers had to say; only the occasional clenching of his ham-like fists betrayed the emotion that rode him. It was as though he held something in his hands that was alive and which he was trying to kill.

"I was coming down from Prescott on other business, Carl, and I thought you might want to know," Powers said.

Dirkes' ice blue eyes stabbed at the lawyer. "You wouldn't be fool enough to get her a divorce, Fred?"

"I put her off. I got out a form and let her sign it. I warned her that it wouldn't be easy, that you'd fight it. It was a good thing she didn't know I was your man, Carl; otherwise she would have gone elsewhere. She might have succeeded, too. She said she had evidence against you, all written down."

"The only way she can get rid of me," Dirkes said harshly, "is to die."

"That's what I told her. I told her that untimely death was the only thing that could separate the two of you."

Carl gave him a shrewd look. "You didn't suggest that the untimely death could be mine?"

"Don't be a fool, Carl. I'm your man, bought and paid for. I'm betraying a confidence in telling you this: a cardinal sin for a lawyer."

"Did she say what evidence she had against me?"

"She may be onto some of your deals, Carl. I heard about the hijacking of the gold from your men the other day. That was mighty careless work, Carl. Folger is taking too many chances."

"One of the hijackers has been killed, Fred. We'll kill the other one on sight, and that will be that," Dirkes growled.

"But you didn't get the gold back, did you?"

"It will turn up."

"Maybe it has already turned up—in the federal marshal's office. Wilma could be in with the hijackers. She might even have hired them."

"I'll handle things here like always, Fred. What are you doing down here in Sabado?"

"A young fellow with a smooth face and faded red hair came to see me. He said he had a mining deal coming up and might need a lawyer. He wanted references."

"What was his name?"

"Brad Regan."

Dirkes exploded a low oath. 'That smooth pilgrim is up to something. He looks like a white-livered kid, but I think he's something more. I don't know of a gold mine around here worth a nickel, or I'd buy it myself."

"What would you do with it, Carl? It's easier to steal gold than to mine it." Fred Powers chuckled, and his Adam's apple bobbed up and down.

"We could use it for a front to get rid of the gold I've got hidden here. We can't go on swapping it for stuff in Mexico. If we had a mine that had any gold in it at all, we could put up a stamp mill, mix the stolen gold with the muck and then smelt it out again."

"That's a lot of trouble to go to."

"But it would be a good cover-up. I've been thinking about it for a long time."

"Suppose they stop shipping gold from Las Cruces?"

"There's enough gold moving out of Tombstone and Bisbee to make it pay off. See if you can locate the man who has the mine to sell."

"Whatever you say, Carl."

Then Carl Dirkes seemed to undergo a metamorphosis. His iron-hard face softened, and a poignant look came to his ice-blue eyes.

"Are you sure that pilgrim didn't get to Wilma?"

"Brad Regan? I don't think so. Why?"

"He was here at the Sabado Bar on a Saturday night. Got in a shooting scrape with Finney. Finney shot him in the head, but he was only creased. Wilma made a big fuss over him. Then in church she used him to shame and anger me."

"I didn't see them together. She went to stay with friends, and he stayed at the hotel. I don't think she knew he was in town. He didn't come in on the stage; he rode in."

"Fred, why does Wilma try to hurt and bedevil me? She's the only woman that I really wanted. I took Felicitas because I like spice and fire in a woman, but she turned out to be a devil. Wilma doesn't fight me openly, but she does little things to spite me, like adopting that puny boy of hers. I want a son of my own, but I'm denied that somehow. Now she wants to adopt a waif, a girl with a questionable background. I give her all the money she asks for."

"Carl, there's some things you can't buy. I've got another piece of news to take your mind off Wilma. I'm attorney for the Cattlemen's Association, as you know, and Bud Wilson has put in a request for a special cattle count. He claims he's losing cows to long-ropers."

"Not to me," Carl said firmly.

"Suppose Folger and Veldon have a side line? They could funnel Wilson cattle through your place, and if they're caught, they could blame the rustling on you."

"You're supposing too much, Fred," Dirkes said, but he had the look of a harassed man. "Go see about the mine."

As Tony walked through the door from the shop into the parlor, Veldon jumped up, his thick legs braced and his blond head thrust forward. His right arm was in a sling, and he wore no gun. Tony resented both facts. He could not fight a one-armed man either with or without a gun.

"What the devil you doing here, Regan?" Veldon barked.

"I'm asking you the same. You're a skunk hiding a cloak of respectability, but you can't disguise your smell. Get out of here and stay away from Ruby Miller."

"Why—why, you big-talk buzzard, you—you kissed her! It shows on yore mouth. Ain't no saddle tramp givin' me that kind of lip. I'll kill you with one hand!"

In his fury, Veldon lifted a chair with his one powerful arm and charged at Tony. Tony took the downsweep of the chair on his back and brushed it off. Then, with one hand behind him to even the fight, Tony charged. He struck Veldon two swift, punishing blows in the guts. Veldon gasped for breath, the air wheezing in his thick throat. Before he could get his wind back, Tony struck him under the chin snapping his head back. Veldon fell, striking his head against the leg of the sofa. He lay limp, still struggling for breath in his unconsciousness.

"Have—you killed him?" Ruby gasped.

"Not him. He'll take a lot more killin' than that, honey." The endearment came easily to his lips.

"You don't know what you've done, Tony. I shouldn't have called you that; he might have heard," she said quickly.

"He didn't hear. What have I done?"

"You've signed your own death warrant."

"I doubt that. Vern will want the satisfaction of killing me himself. He can't do that until his arm is out of the sling."

"But he can. He can shoot as well with either hand, darl—Brad."

"Say what you were going to, Ruby."

"I haven't got the right."

"Between us we can win the right, honey. Say it."

"Darling," she said dutifully.

Tony felt a rush of feeling at the sound of the word on her lips. He could not remember ever having the same depth of feeling for Wilma.

"I like the sound of it," he said, but he forced himself not to kiss her. His emotions were in too much of a turmoil to commit himself hastily. Taking Veldon's good arm, he dragged him through the kitchen and out into the alley at the rear. Ruby followed him, her face white with fear.

"He won't bother you until after he kills me," Tony told her. "Keep your back door locked."

Tony dipped some water from the stagnant rain barrel and threw it into Veldon's face. Then he turned on his heel and went out onto the main drag. Mounting his horse, he rode first to the express office and found the agent going over some accounts. The agent looked up when Tony entered the waiting room.

"Hey, you," he said. "You're that Brad Regan that

was askin' me all them questions the other day, ain't you?"

"One and the same."

"Ain't you a little scared to show yoreself hereabouts? The stage was robbed the day after you got so nosy. Reckon I ought to have you arrested pronto as a suspect."

"Hold it there." Tony grinned. "Not guilty."

"Of course you'd say that."

Tony decided to take a chance.

"Can you keep your mouth about company business, Lukens?" Tony had seen the agent's name on the manifest.

"I ain't never been accused of talkin' too much."

Tony took out his special agent's badge and showed it to Lukens.

"Well, I'll be hornswaggled," Lukens said, scratching his head. "You sure had me fooled."

"Have you any idea who might tip off the gang when the gold is leaving Las Cruces, Lukens?"

"Like I told you, I don't even know myself."

"When will the driver and the guard who were held up the other day be going through here again?"

"Couple of days, mebbe. They'll be goin' back to Las Cruces."

"Thanks, Lukens. Don't let on that you know me."

Tony mounted once more. It was getting late when he headed for Honkytown. This not being Saturday, the saloons would not be crowded. He hoped to find Pop Smith in town, making his brag about his gold strike. He wasn't disappointed. He found Pop in the Red Garter, buying drinks for the house. He was relieved to find neither Folger or Veldon here. Veldon was no doubt nursing a headache somewhere in Holytown; he hoped it wasn't at Ruby Miller's. Folger was no doubt out on the range or at the Box-X. He did spy a man with his shoulder bandaged and recognized him as the robber he had shot during the hijacking. He had his partner with him. Tony bellied up to the bar next to Pop, who let out a whoop when he saw him.

"Well, dog my cats, if it ain't Brad Regan!" the bent old man exclaimed, sleeving the beer off his beard. "Have a drink on me, younker."

"You act like a man who's struck it rich," Tony said, winking at Pop.

"I'm cuttin' you in, boy. You put me on the track of the gold when you was out to my mine."

"I might buy you out, old-timer," Tony said, ordering a beer.

"Already got a buyer lined up. That lawyer man, Fred Powers from Prescott, he cornered me and took me to see Carl Dirkes. Dirkes is lookin' fer a gold mine."

"Is he buying sight unseen?"

"Nope. I wouldn't sell thataway. He offered me five thousand sight unseen. I told him he'd better come to the mine and make sure the gold's there, and then we'll talk price."

"What did he say?"

"We're goin' up tomorrow, me an' him an' the lawyer feller. Why don't you come along?"

"Maybe I will," Tony said.

Somebody else got Pop's attention, so Tony slid his beer down the bar until he was next to the man with the wounded arm.

"I'm Brad Regan, pardner. Looks like you ran into some bad luck."

"Got hooked by a steer's horn while tryin' to bull-dog him."

"You working around here?"

"We work for Dirkes when he needs extra hands. Other times Asp boy, here—" he nodded to the man near him—"works in the stamp mill at Las Cruces. I swamp out at the stage depot when there's nothing better." He added, "It don't pay much."

"Pays better than robbing stages, the way I hear." Tony grinned.

The wounded man tensed. "What do you mean by that?"

"I hear tell the robbers was robbed by some hijackers. The hijackers got the gold, and they got a good look at the robbers. That complicates things. The hijackers not only got the gold, but they can turn the robbers in and collect a reward."

"They won't live so long. I hear Folger already killed one of them."

"How would Folger know it was one of them,

Charley?"

Charley said to his pardner, "Asp, you talk too much."

"Who was the man he killed?"

"The way I hear it, Folger shot the man and knocked him out of the saddle. The hombre's hoss bolted, and Folger chased it. When he finally caught it, there was no gold in the saddlebags."

"The man couldn't by chance have been an Apache Indian?"

"Folger couldn't tell."

"Because he shot him in the back, is that it?" Tony said grimly.

"Who in blazes are you?" Asp demanded. "You talk like the law, with all them questions."

"Just interested."

The men clammed up, and Tony moved back beside Pop. The story Folger told about the shooting didn't make much sense. If Abe's horse had bolted, then how had Abe been able to ride it back to the ranch? It was possible that Abe's horse was loyal enough to return to his master. On the other hand, it was more likely that Folger had shot Abe from ambush and knew who he was, and also had a good idea who his partner had been. The thought made Tony uneasy. Vern Veldon had already vowed to kill him. If Folger suspected him of being one of the hijackers, he would have to kill him to protect himself. But first Folger would make sure he got the gold back, relying on the silence of the hijackers because of their own crime.

Tony got a room at the Honkytown hotel, and the following morning he met Pop Smith, Dirkes, and Fred Powers outside the Sabado Queen. Dirkes frowned when Tony rode up.

"What are you doing here, Regan?" Dirkes barked.

Pop said quickly, "I cut him in on the deal. He made me an offer on the mine in case you don't buy it. Best offer takes the works. We need Brad there to help with the drillin' an blastin'. I ain't goin' to sell you a pig in a poke."

"Such honesty is refreshing," Dirkes said with a slight sneer.

"You three go ahead and inspect the mine. I've got business here in town. I'm not much of a mining man, anyway," Fred Powers said.

When they reached the mine above Galena, they went immediately to work. Pop brought out the box of powder, which looked as though it had never been opened, and pried the top off. Tony filled a sack with sticks of powder, cut some seven-foot lengths of time fuse and clamped a detonator on the end of each length of fuse. Pop carried the fuses, a dozen of them; Tony carried the dynamite; and Dirkes carried a gold pan and a shovel.

"Pop can explain the formation better than I can," Tony said.

"I ran onto this old buried stream bed jest a week ago," Pop said. "I reckon ages ago, it was a river on

top of the ground. Got buried and dried up when the
ground faulted through an earthquake. The gold got
buried in the gravel during the thousands of years the
river was alive. The water dried up, but the gold
stayed here."

They passed a crosscut in the tunnel and soon came
to the face of the rock. Pop had run a crosscut along
the face of the gravel, exposing it for about thirty feet.
They stuck their candlesticks with the lighted candles
into cracks in the wall. Tony picked out a sharp drill
from the pile stored in the tunnel and picked up a single
jack with which to drive the drill into the gravel.

"This is loose ground," Tony said as he began ham-
mering on the steel drill. "It shouldn't take more than
a stick to a hole. We'll blast one hole at a time all along
the face of the gravel deposit to see if the dust is
consistent."

Dirkes made no comment; just watched the proceedings with a stony face. Tony loaded the first hole, lit
the fuse, and they retreated into the crosscut farther
back in the drift. When the stick of dynamite exploded,
it jarred the earth, and the concussion almost broke
their eardrums. Pop took the gold pan as soon as the
smoke from the blast had subsided, and went to the
pile of muck the dynamite had torn loose. He shoveled
up some of the muck into the pan, and they all went
to the spring outside the mine. Here he washed the rock
with a practiced hand, and sure enough, there was three
or four dollars' worth of gold in the pan.

Pop said, "This ain't much of a test, but it proves the gold is thar. If a man had a stamp mill, he might break a lot of gold out of them big rocks."

They repeated the performance until the dynamite was used up, and each shot showed up about the same amoun of gold, because of the amount planted in the dynamite. A more experienced miner might have been suspicious of such consistency, but Dirkes showed only an ill-concealed satisfaction. Later, when they were in the cabin eating some of Pop's venison and baked potatoes, Dirkes began to dicker.

"You've got gold here, all right, but it's a slow producer. I'll give you ten thousand dollars for the mine."

"Twenty-five thousand," Pop said promptly.

"Are you crazy?" Dirkes said. "You've been living alone too long."

"You offered me five thousand sight unseen."

"Fifteen thousand," Dirkes said grumpily.

"Thirty thousand," Pop said.

"It's robbery, but I'll give you twenty."

"How about that, Brad?"

"It's your mine."

"I'll take it." Pop offered his hand.

Dirkes shook on it.

In the bank at Sabado, Pop Smith signed a quit-claim deed, and Dirkes gave him a draft for twenty thousand dollars which he promptly cashed. Fred Powers was there to guide the proceedings, and Tony heard him say to Dirkes as they went out the door: "I hope you didn't throw that money down a rat-hole."

Tony led Pop over to Ruby's place, and in her parlor they divided up the money.

"Has Veldon been bothering you since yesterday?" Tony asked her.

"No, but I saw him around town this morning, and he's wearing a gun. I'm afraid for you, dar—darling." She hesitated over the word.

"Look, honey, I've got my strength back. I never lost my fast draw; I'll be all right."

"I've leave you two lovebirds alone," Pop said. "I aim to buy me a new outfit, find me that ranch in the sun, and sit there and bake the rheumatiz' outa my bones. You both come an' see me sometime."

When Pop had gone, Tony tied his share of the money in a bundle and pushed it toward Ruby.

"Can you hide this for me, Carrots?"

"Of course, but why?"

"On second thought, you'd better not. If anybody suspected you had the money, they would turn the place upside down. Ten thousand dollars is a big sum. I'll take it over to Lupe; they won't suspect her."

"I'm no coward, Brad."

"I know that, but they might torture you to make you tell. I couldn't have that," Tony said with feeling.

"I have a gun, too," Ruby said firmly.

"I've got an idea. Get me some old newspapers and your dressmaking shears."

"What for, Brad?"

"I aim to cut up enough paper to make a bundle the size of the money and take it with me."

"I'll cut it up for you. Do you want it plain or hem-stitched?" She laughed.

He watched her expert hands wield the shears, and he knew that here was a woman who needed a home, a husband and family to care for. He wrapped the fake money in a paper.

"Where will you hide the real money?" he asked her, still worried.

"Don't trust me, is that it?" She smiled.

"I'd trust you with my life, Carrots," he said.

"But with money, you're afraid I may abscond?"

"No teasing; this is serious."

"I have a hiding place no one can find. Don't worry about me. You let Pop go out of here with his money."

"That's different. Pop's a cagey old-timer, used to taking care of himself," Tony assured her.

She stood close to him, looking up into his eyes. "They might threaten *me* to make *you* tell them where the money is. If you don't know, you can't give it to them."

"That's no comfort to me at all, honey." He permitted himself one gentle kiss before he left.

The news of the mine deal swept across the town like the wind. Men looked at Tony and talked to him and eyed the bundle of what they thought was money. He was deliberately making sure nobody would suspect the money was in Ruby's shop, well hidden. He rode through Honkytown on his way to the ranch and even stopped for a drink in the Red Garter, laying the package carelessly on the bar. He saw a man disappear out the back door and knew his bait had been swallowed. He could now ride to the ranch and let out a rumor that the money was hidden there.

The sun was low as he started on the twenty-mile ride to the ranch; it would be dark before he got there. Near the halfway mark, he had to ride through the low sand hills and the thick growth of brush at Cherry Creek. He tensed as he studied the shadows on either side of the road. He could be riding into an ambush; an ambush prepared by somebody who believed he carried ten thousand dollars in cash.

He stopped under a low hanging tree to let his horse drink as he crossed the creek, and he was unprepared for the attack that came from the sky. A form leaped out of the tree, caught him around the neck and dragged him from the saddle. He hit the ground rolling and kicking out to free himself of the tenacious fingers that caught his throat. Even in the dusk he made out the face of the man called "Asp" to whom he had talked in the Red Garter the day before. The packet of phony money fell from his shirt pocket into the water.

Tony tore himself loose and crouched to his feet. Asp came at him, head down like a bull. Tony put up a knee that smashed the man's face. He turned around as Asp, cursing and groaning with pain, straightened up. Asp tried to get at his gun, but it had slid from the holster in the wild attack. He came at Tony, his arms pumping like pistons. Tony felt the blows bruise his ribs and rock his head. He concentrated on Asp's face, beating it mercilessly. Then Asp backed off and made a sudden lunge. Tony side-stepped the lunge, and Asp's momentum caused him to lose his footing and land face down in the water. Tony pounced on him and held his head under the water.

"Did Dirkes send you out here to steal his money back?" Tony demanded.

Tony, straddling Asp's back, pulled his head out of the water so he could talk.

"No!" Asp blubbered.

Down went his head again.

"Who sent you?"

"Nobody!"

Down went his head, and this time it stayed until the man's struggles were feeble twitches. Then Tony pulled his head out and waited while he gasped and sputtered until he could speak.

"I'll talk, you buzzard. You meant to kill me!"

"You started the ruckus. Talk."

Tony still had his fingers wound in Asp's thick hair.

"Veldon sent me. He wanted to come himself, but he's got a bum arm."

While Tony had Asp in a talking mood, he plied him for information.

"Who is the tip-off man at Las Cruces, who tells you

when the gold is going out?"

"What makes you think I'd know that?"

"I was the other hijacker."

"You what? Man, you're askin' for death. I don't mind tellin' you anything you want. You won't live long enough to use it. You're a crook, too. You got the gold. You're fair game for any gun. Charley, my pard, he's the tip-off man."

Tony's gun had not gone under water. He drew it now and let the half-drowned Asp get to his feet.

"Fork your hoss and ride, Asp. Tell Veldon to take care of his own dirty work."

"Do I get my gun?"

Tony picked Asp's gun out of the water and, as an added precaution, snapped the shells out of it before he tossed it to the cowed crook.

"I wouldn't be in your shoes, pilgrim," he said as he dried his face with a bandana, which was also wet, and rode away.

Reaching the ranch, Tony dismounted at the big house. It was dark now, and he knocked on the door twice before getting an answer. The door swung open, and Bud Wilson stood in the yellow square of light.

"Come in," Wilson said grimly.

"How's Abe?" were Tony's first words.

"He's still alive. He was conscious for a few minutes and spoke to Lucy. He confirmed the fact that Folger shot him. He says Dirkes thinks that I sent out the hijackers to take the gold away from his men."

"I heard you sent for an Association inspector to check Dirkes' range?"

"Dirkes is figuring to cut me down. I don't intend to take it without a fight. The inspector should be here in a couple of days."

"I want to be on the inspection cavvy," Tony said flatly.

"You've surprised me, boy, ever since I first laid eyes on you in Lupe's Café. If you want to be on the cavvy, it's fine with me."

"Thanks. May I see Abe?"

Wilson led the way to the back bedroom. Lucy came out of the door, wide-eyed.

"He came to again, and he's fuming to get out of bed," she said.

CHAPTER TEN

That night Tony avoided the bunkhouse. He wanted to avoid Baudry and Fats, because they might have learned the truth from Folger. He was not ready for those two men yet. If everything else turned out all right, they could be prosecuted for cattle rustling later. He wondered what side they'd be on in a showdown. He went, unseen, to the cook shack after the men had eaten and asked Chow Lee to let him sleep in the flunky bunk off the kitchen.

"Where you go allee time, Blad? You no worth your chow."

"Business, Chow Lee. Private business."

"You makee private business here, chop chop."

"Some men want to kill me, Chow Lee."

"No dinghou, no good! You some kind lawman, Blad?"

Tony took a chance and showed Chow Lee his badge. The Chinese was greatly impressed.

"We've got to keep it a secret for a few days, Chow Lee."

"My lips tight like Buddha. No speak. Dwung

ro—stew, hot on stove. You eat. Sleep here. Chow Lee be watchdog."

Tony was up before daylight when not a soul was stirring but Chow Lee, who started breakfast early. Chow Lee insisted on giving him ham and eggs and plenty of hot coffee, and he also wrapped up some biscuits and cold meat for Tony to take with him.

"You go catchee clooks, you need plenty food," Chow Lee told him.

Tony got his horse from behind the haystack where he had tied him the night before and headed north on the Tall-W range. It was daylight before he reached the place where the fence had been cut, and he saw the tracks of cattle going through the fence. He let himself through the fence, crossed the barranca, and picked up the tracks on the other side on Box-X range. He followed the tracks across broken country, trying not to be seen, and reached a flat section of sage interspersed liberally with bunch grass, which, though dry at this time of year, was very nourishing. He began to run across bunches of cows on which the Tall-W brand had been clumsily changed to a Box-X. This was what he wanted; this was where the inspection could start.

He was at a loss to understand why the brand-blotting had been done so carelessly. Baudry's story was that Folger wanted the stolen cattle found so as to start a range war between Dirkes and Wilson; then Folger and his gang could step in and take over. Dirkes wasn't averse to stealing cattle; he stole from everybody he could.

If he spared Wilson, it was only to keep Wilson on his side until he didn't need him any more. It was dead certain that Carl Dirkes would not rest until he was top dog of the whole range.

It was noon when Tony turned back, satisfied with his discovery. On the way back he swung around by the homestead he had been cheated of and, staking his horse in the hollow that held the spring which made the land valuable, walked back to the cabin with his package of food under his arm. There was still a bench in the cabin and a table he had built himself. Cobwebs festooned the corners of the rustic interior, and a trade rat darted from the nest in the old straw of the corner bunk.

As he ate his cold meal, Tony let his fancy wander. So absorbed was he in his thoughts, he did not hear the slow approach of a horse. He should have been alert to every sound, considering the danger he was in, but his thoughts were turned inward, to the hollow place where his dreams had been. His wits were alerted by the sound of a voice—no, not a voice—the sound of a woman sobbing. He sat stiff and bewildered. Had his nostalgia been so deep and absorbing that it had become real? He must be losing his mind. He rose and walked to the cabin door.

At first he still thought it was his imagination. Wilma Dirkes could not be sitting there staring back at him, her mouth agape and her eyes shiny with tears. But she was there, as surprised as he by the sudden confrontation. She was seated like a queen on her buckskin horse, her saddle bright with silver and her red silk shirt a blazing banner.

"Good God," she said, her words a prayer, "what are you doing here, Brad?"

"I might ask you the same thing," he said gently, still spellbound by her appearance.

"This is Bar-X range. It has the Bar-X curse on it, the same as I. You are trespassing."

"I stopped only to eat my lunch."

"But you hid your horse."

"I tethered him on grass in the hollow by the spring." Tony explained, adding, "I'm a marked man, didn't you know that? Finney, the undertaker, has a grudge against me. Then there's Folger. He couldn't quite defeat me, so he's afraid, and I have a broad back. There's your religious, respectable husband, who hates me because you cater to me. Are you trying to make him mad enough to kill me?"

"God forbid!" she said fervently. "Since you came to town, I'm all churned up inside. You weaken my resolve; you bring back memories of another day. I might have lived in this shack. Do you realize that?"

"You were lucky to escape such humiliation and drudgery."

"I traded it for hell and damnation to save a man's life."

Her last words shocked Tony to the soles of his feet. There was a hidden meaning there that he didn't understand.

"So you come out here to gloat over your good fortune at having escaped the miseries of a pioneer life?"

A tear formed and trickled down her cheek. She didn't wipe it away.

"I'm gloating so much it brings tears to my eyes," she said in a choking voice. "I often come here to live with ghosts. Nobody knows the truth, and I can't speak up. If I did, I'd be either a victim of self-pity, or a woman who sold her soul to the devil."

Tony felt his own throat choking up and wanted to put his arms about her and lift her from the saddle. He didn't dare touch her. She was Mrs. Carl Dirkes, they were alone, and to feel her in his arms on this spot he had once consecrated to her would be more than flesh could stand.

"Why don't you come inside and tell me about it? There's a bench inside."

"For some reason, you make me want to confide in you, Brad. Being surrounded by crooks and mountebanks, I have locked my heart and mind against the world, but you make me want to open it."

"You might feel better if you did."

"Maybe you're right, but my horse could be seen from a distance."

"I'll take him to the hollow with my horse, Extrano. Nobody will see him there."

With the horses out of sight, and hidden by the cabin walls, Tony and Wilma sat down with three feet separating them. Tony wanted it that way; he couldn't trust himself to be closer to her lest his emotion betray him. This was where they would have lived as man and wife, and now they were strangers. He tried to stop the tumult in his heart, so as not to blind his eyes to reality. She was not the same impulsive Wilma he had known; she had matured, and there was a hardness about her mouth and a glowing resentment in her large eyes. If things could be changed back to what they were, the hardness and resentment might vanish. But could things ever be changed; could time be turned backward?

"I did a foul thing once, but it was unintentional," she began, and a slight shudder went through her. "I knew a young man once, scarcely more than an impetuous boy. He was in love with me."

"And you have no feeling for him?"

"I *had* more feeling for him than people knew," she said fiercely. "It was because of my love for him that I destroyed him."

Tony felt a chill go through him. The ghosts of the past were laying their cold hands upon the present. She was talking in riddles, and he waited for her to explain them.

"I don't understand," Tony said. "You destroyed the man you loved. I thought only black widow spiders did that."

"Don't judge me until you hear me out. Carl Dirkes was after Tony Egan's land; he rustled his few cattle;

he was after me. He ordered Tony Egan off his homestead because it had valuable water on it. Tony defied Carl, dared Carl to run him off. It was working up to a showdown between Dirkes and Tony Egan. Tony was fast with a gun; he had an even chance to kill Carl. I talked him out of it. I went to Carl, and he agreed to talk the thing over if Tony would come to his house.

"Tony agreed reluctantly to please me, and he took Patch Roger, his buddy, along with him. They were ambushed in Dirkes' ranch yard. In the mix-up Tony accidentally killed Patch, or so the witnesses said."

"Whose witnesses?"

"Carl's men; they were the only ones there. Tony attacked Carl, and Carl shot him. Then Tony was beaten and stomped until his face was a gruesome mask."

"And you married a man who did that?"

"Carl denied he did it; he blamed it on his men. Tony escaped to Mexico and recovered from the bullet wound, but Carl had him extradited and tried for the murder of Patch Roger. The witnesses were on Carl's side; there was no one to defend Tony. Carl insisted on first degree murder and a hanging. That way Tony could bother him no more. Then I did the only thing I could think of to right in some measure the wrong I had done. Carl said he would agree to a charge of manslaughter and a ten-year prison term if I would marry him."

Tony sat there digesting this like a man made of stone. She had married Carl Dirkes to save him from a rope! The realization of how great her sacrifice had been struck him with sickening force. She had sold her-self in desperation to save the man she loved.

"So that's how it was," he said softly. "You've been living with him, heckling him, undermining him and using his money for good deeds. It reads more like a novel, Wilma, than a true story." He sat rigid, the three feet of space still between them. He had to learn all there was to learn about Dirkes' evil deeds. "I read the book in the drawer of your dressing table at the Sabado Queen when I took my poker money out. Where did you get your information?"

"You couldn't be a lawman by any chance, could you?"

"Not exactly." He showed her his special agent's badge. "I'm working on the stage line, trying to stop the robberies that have gone on periodically."

"Brad Regan, special agent," she said softly. "I learned the combination to my husband's safe. I have seen his records."

"Where does he keep the stolen gold until he can dispose of it?"

"He hides it in a cistern near the house, under the scummy water."

"You're taking your life in your hands, Wilma, telling me this."

"It makes no difference—or it soon won't. I'll be gone."

Then a thought struck Tony, something that had stuck

in his craw since his visit to Prescott.

"It couldn't have been you who filed for divorce with Lawyer Powers?"

"Why not?"

"Because Carl would never let you go. He'd kill you first. Powers is Carl's lawyer, too, and ethics wouldn't stop him from telling Carl your intentions. What would you do if you were divorced?"

Wilma rose and paced the puncheon floor. "I have heard that Tony Egan has been released from prison. His sentence was cut short. He would go some place where nobody knew him because of his hideous face. I would try to find him and make up to him for the wrong I did."

Tony felt a sudden surge of compassion for the troubled woman. He leaped up and confronted her, putting his hands on her shoulders and looking into her brooding eyes.

"You won't have to look for Tony Egan," he said softly. "I am Tony Egan."

The look in her eyes turned to one almost of hate. "I'm in no mood for jokes, Brad."

"You said you had a feeling about me since I came here," he persisted gravely. "Trust your feelings. My prison term was cut down because I volunteered for a medical experiment called plastic surgery. My face was made over, my nose straightened."

"How can this be true?" she asked, her lips trembling.

"Ask Ruby Miller; she knows me."

Then the floodgates burst, and the pent-up emotions of five long years were submerged in the torrent of belief and acceptance that swept over her. She almost fainted at his feet, and Tony caught her in his arms. She clung to him, her head against his breast, shaken by the sobs that were torn from the very core of her being.

"Wal, now, this is something," a jeering voice said from the doorway where there was no door.

Tony stiffened at the sound, his emotions immune from further shock. He turned his head and saw Kent Wilson staring at him while he held Carl Dirkes' wife in his arms.

"What are you doing here, Kent?" Tony said in a deadly voice.

"I was ridin' up north. I stopped at the spring for a drink and saw Extrano there, and the buckskin. Nobody rides a fancy rig like was on that hoss but Mrs. Dirkes. I thought I'd stop and say hello." He grinned.

Wilma, stifling her sobs, raised her tear-stained face and looked at Kent.

"This is not what you're thinking it is at all, Kent Wilson," she said.

"What are I thinking, Mrs. Dirkes? I heard tell you cozied up to this cowboy in church."

"We met here accidentally, Kent," Tony said in a hard voice. "Don't go making trouble out of it."

"Some accident," Kent said, the stiff smile still on

his lips. "I ain't young as you might think. When a man squeezes a woman to him—"

"Shut up before you say too much, Kent!" Tony said in a voice that stopped the kid cold. He released Wilma and went menacingly toward the boy on the horse. A look of fright crossed the kid's face, and he dug spurs to his horse and raced away.

"I'm sorry, Tony," Wilma said, burying her face in her hands. "I will always be a jinx to you. When the town is told that we *sneaked* up here to an abandoned shack to keep a tryst, Carl will hear of it and will kill us both."

"Not you, Wilma. He won't kill you as long as he owns you. He loves you in his own way, and he doesn't understand that love. He knows only that he needs you; he needs the kind of a thing you are, a soft, loving, giving spirit to make the rest of his life bearable. He would kill you only if he realized he had lost you completely."

"Tony—" she looked up at him, her eyes pleading— "what are we going to do?"

"I don't rightly know. But know this. I didn't kill Patch; Dirkes did."

"I can't ask you to take me back after what I did to you."

"You don't have to ask it, Wilma." He had wanted to say darling, but the word stuck in his throat because he had so lately used it with Ruby. He had never dreamed that he would expose himself to Wilma so soon. Her tragic story had loosened his tongue. She had sacrificed her own happiness to save him from being hanged by the neck until dead. That thought stuck in his mind. It boiled down to the fact that he owed her his life. What could he deny her if she asked it? It was no longer just a question of love; it was a question of loyalty and reparation.

"I'm going home, Tony, before Carl hears about this. I'd rather tell him myself how Brad Regan found me fainting in the cabin and helped me."

"He knows you're well and strong."

"I'll tell him I'm going to have a baby, anything to keep him from killing you, Tony."

"Tell him nothing, Wilma, not for a couple of days. He may never hear about us. I think I can stop Kent from talking."

"I've got to go; it's getting late," she said.

When Tony got back from the spring with the horses, they mounted, and he kissed her goodbye. It was a lingering kiss, but it lacked something. Had it been blunted by her fear, or by his knowledge that she was unattainable?

He reached the ranch after dark, his mind a jumble of thoughts. If Wilma were free, if by some turn of events, divorce or otherwise, Carl Dirkes had no claim or control on her, what would he, Tony, do? He would have to accept her because of what had happened and try to recreate the love and ambitions they had once had. He could do nothing less unless she rejected him.

At the ranch he skirted the bunkhouse and rode up to the big house, tying his horse behind the well house out of sight. Kate Wilson, a smile on her lined face, greeted him at the door.

"Come in, come in, Brad," she said. "Maybe you can talk some sense into that black man's head."

"What's the matter with him?"

"He insists he's well enough to get out of bed and ride a horse."

"Unconscious a couple of days ago, and now raring to go, eh?"

"The wound isn't as bad as we thought. The doctor was here today. The bullet knocked him unconscious, but it didn't penetrate his head. Come on and talk to him."

As he went through the house, Tony looked for Kent, but he was nowhere to be seen. Abe, in the back bedroom, was propped up in bed, his neck swathed in a bandage which did not impede his speech. He was arguing with Lucy at the foot of the bed.

"Yo'all jest fetch me mah britches, chile, an' I'll traipse on outa heah. Yo' done made enough fuss ovah mah black hide. I kin take care of mahself, personal, down in mah bunk. Chow Lee can fetch me vittles."

"Talk to this crazy coot," Lucy said to Tony. "The doctor says he has to stay in bed another day or two to make sure the concussion doesn't return. A blood clot could be forming on what little brain he was."

"You can't move tonight, pardner," Tony said. "I'll

tell you what I'll do. I'll sleep on that other cot over there tonight, and the women won't have to worry about you." He indicated the cot against the other wall.

"Good," Lucy said. "Have you had any supper?"

"No, but I'll go get some from Chow Lee."

"You won't. We've got plenty left over. I like to look after my own man."

"Lucy, you're a tease." Tony grinned, but her possessive threats irked him. "Have you see Kent tonight?"

"He was at supper."

"Did he have any special news?"

"A brother wouldn't give a sister the time of day."

At least Kent had not spread his secret news at home. Tony listened to Lucy's chatter while he ate, and later talked to Mr. Wilson about what he had found on Bar-X range. He learned the Association Rep would be there in two days, and he wondered if the man's secret check was known to Dirkes. If it was, why hadn't Dirkes moved the rustled cattle off his range? Did Dirkes feel confident that he could buck all the cattlemen in the territory, or was what Baudry had told him the truth? Maybe Folger *had* rigged the deal to get Carl and Bud Wilson at each other's throats so that he and his cronies could pick up the pieces.

After turning his horse into the small corral near the house where the family horses were kept and fed, Tony went to bed in Abe's room, wondering why Kent had not come home. Could he be down in the bunkhouse with the men, giving them his piece of juicy gossip? Then another thought disturbed him. Kent could have heard part of the conversation with Wilma in the cabin and learned his true identity. If Dirkes knew that Brad Regan was really Tony Egan come back to haunt him, he would turn the guns loose and offer a reward for Tony Egan's hide.

Tony was up before anybody was stirring. In the semi-darkness of the bedroom, Abe was snoring gently. Tony let himself out of the house without awaking anybody and, forking his horse, began the two-hour ride to town. There were things he had to do before the showdown.

In town, he went to the stage office and got pencil, paper and envelope from Lukens. He wrote a letter to Handley in Prescott. He named the stage robbers, the lookout man who informed them when the gold would be shipped, and warned that the driver and shotgun guard might be part of the gang. He told where the stolen gold was hidden in the cistern. He sealed the letter with wax and gave it to Lukens.

"If anything happens to me, Lukens, please see that Handley, the district superintendent at Prescott, gets this letter. If I pull through, I'll take it to him myself."

He passed Ruby's shop on his way to Lupe's for breakfast, and was puzzled to see the door closed and the blinds drawn. He decided she had slept in and, not wishing to disturb her, he went on into Lupe's. There were several men having breakfast there, late eaters such as the banker and Dr. Deadmer. Tony only half heard the conversation.

"You no *trabajo* very much, *Señor* Brad. You no work like the other vaqueros. All the time in town. Ruby Meeler, I think she sweet on you. You her *querido*, sweetheart?" Lupe asked before taking his order.

Tony grinned. "Lupe, I didn't know you were a matchmaker. We're friends, that's all."

Lupe winked. "*Buenos amigos,* eh? Keesing type *amigos?*"

Tony said, "Bring me some ham and eggs, Lupe. I'm not good enough for Ruby."

"You theenk maybe thees Veldon hombre more better?"

"He won't bother her again. I gave him some advice."

"Ver' good advice, *amigo.* She tell me."

Lupe walked toward the kitchen, swinging her ample hips, and Tony became aware of the conversation. At first he thought he had misunderstood; Smith was a common name. But when he heard the name Pop Smith, he turned to look at Dr. Deadmer, who was doing the talking.

"They brought the old-timer in, but there was nothing I could do for him. It appears that his burro which he was riding, slipped off the trail in Devil's Canyon and fell into the bottom of the gorge. Killed him outright."

For a moment Tony couldn't speak; a wave of anger and hate churned through him.

"Did he have any money on him, Doc?" Tony got the words out.

"Not that I know of. There was no mention of money."

"Everybody knew he sold his mine. He had ten thousand dollars on him."

"It could have been that the money fell out of his pocket or his pack on the way down."

Tony saw it all, and a cold fury possessed him. Dirkes had given in too easily on the mine deal. He had dickered just enough to make it look like a deal. All along he had meant to steal the money back once he got control of the mine. Pop, on the eve of achieving his life's dream, was dead, and Tony felt partially guilty for his death because he had engineered the deal.

"He didn't fall off the cliff with his burro," Tony said coldly. "He was murdered."

"How do you know that, Regan?"

"Pop never rode on Nellie. She carried his pack, but he never asked her to carry him."

CHAPTER ELEVEN

Tony Egan gulped his ham and eggs, feeling an urgent need for action. The man who had killed Pop Smith would have to pay for the cowardly murder. He had a good idea who that man was—Dirkes' right hand man, Blackie Folger. He didn't wait to pay Lupe for his breakfast; she could put it on his bill. He went out into the street and stopped in front of Ruby's shop. The blinds were still drawn over her display window, and, trying the door, he found it locked. Scowling, he went around to the back door and found that locked also. He thought maybe Ruby was being extra careful because of the ten thousand dollars she had in her keeping. Locking the doors and not opening for business as usual, would only attract attention rather than protect her. He knocked on the door but got no response.

He went up the alley to Lupe's kitchen door, let himself into the steamy, odorful room and found Lupe turning flapjacks.

"Have you seen Ruby this morning, Lupe?"

"I have see nothing but the top of the stove and hongry faces."

"She wasn't in for breakfast?"

"Mostly she cooks at her place."

"Did you see her leave the shop with anybody yesterday or last night?"

"No, *amigo*, I see nothing."

"Could she have gone to some woman's house to do a fitting?"

"*Quien sabe?* Why you ask all thees questiones?"

"Her place is locked up and her blinds are still drawn," Tony explained.

"Why don't you push the door open? The lock she is not so strong."

"Thanks, Lupe," he said, going back to the alley. She had been of little help except for her last obvious suggestion. Before testing the door, he knocked again, loudly, but there was no response. A dozen thoughts went through his mind. She could even be lying in the place unconscious. Raising a foot, he drove it into the door near the keeper of the lock. The metal snapped, and the door swung open.

Even in his wildest imaginings Tony had not pictured what his eyes now saw. The kitchen was a shambles, pots and pans strewn about, cupboard doors open and even the flour box turned upside down. With growing apprehension, he went on into the living room to find the furniture turned over and the drawers ransacked. He was almost afraid to look in the bedroom; she could be lying there dead. Trying to control his rising emotions, he opened the bedroom door. He should not have left the money with her, but if he had taken it with him he would have lost it had Asp's attack succeeded. Putting it in the bank would have made it easy for Dirkes to get at it, as he was part owner of the bank. He had had no idea that Ruby would be subjected to such havoc.

The bedroom was empty, the covers on the floor and the mattress turned over. He wondered where Ruby could have hidden the money, and if the thief had found it. His concern deepened when he went into the shop and found dresses and material strewn about. Then his eye caught sight of the note lying on the shop counter. It was printed in large, bold letters:

Regan: I didn't find the money, so you must have it. If you want to see Ruby Miller alive, bring the money to the old mission outside of town. Leave the money in the last room of the wing of the mission that is still standing. Noon is the deadline.

The note was unsigned, but Tony was sure who had printed it. Vern Veldon was getting even with him and Ruby at the same time, and getting the money in the bargain. Fingering his gun, Tony felt a choking hate and fear, hate for Vern Veldon and fear for Ruby. He felt a calm settle over him, a cold, deadly calm. He had a conviction that at the end of this day either he or Vern Veldon would be dead. He went out the back door, fastening the door shut with a piece of wire. He walked to the street and mounted his horse, his face a deadly mask. Mounting Extrano, he rode through the town, and when he saw the ruins huddling out on the desert, he pulled up.

Veldon would be looking for him to hide into a trap, a trap that would be sprung with a death bullet. Like all missions, La Quintada had been built with a large church in the center and wings running from the church to house the personnel, take care of travelers, and provide workshops in which was done weaving, leather work and other things. The main part of the mission had half fallen into rubble, but in one of the wings some of the old rooms were still intact. The windows of the rooms faced the town, and a man riding toward them could be spotted far off. If he rode directly toward the mission, it would be like storming a fort single-handed.

Tony rode into a shallow arroyo, deep enough to hide him from the mission. When he was far to the east of the mission, he cut out through the tall mesquite until he was out of sight of the windows. Then he turned directly toward the blind end of the mission. When he reached the adobe walls, he stopped his horse and, standing in the saddle, managed to scramble up on the low roof. The roof was old, the timbers half rotten, and many of the tiles were missing. The note had said the end room, which was the one under him. Easing his way along, he found a hole in the roof where a tile was missing.

He peered into the room, which was festooned with spider webs and littered with dirt. There was no one there. The note had said to leave the money; it had not said how Ruby was to be released. Veldon must have Ruby in one of the other rooms, and he must be waiting for Tony to walk into the trap. There could be a dozen peepholes through which Veldon could watch the room.

Tony edged his way across the roof, careful to keep on the ridgepole and avoid the rotting rafters. He felt confident that Veldon would not kill him until he had the money. Veldon must have felt sure the money was in Ruby's shop, or he would not have torn the place to pieces as he had. But what could have convinced him that Ruby had the money? Could Asp have gone back after his beating in the creek and told Veldon that he, Tony, had been carrying only cut up paper? Asp might have noticed that if he had seen the bundle in the water with the wrapper washed off. So Veldon had guessed Ruby had the money and, not finding it, meant to force Tony to give up the money in order to save Ruby.

Tony judged he was over the next room of the mission wing, but there was no hole through which he could see into the room. Farther down the roof, toward the wall, there was a hole where the tiles were missing. He decided to chance it, praying that the old rafters would hold his weight. He slid carefully down toward the bare place. Inch by inch he worked his way soundlessly across the tiles. He reached the bare rafters from which the tiles were missing, and as he twisted around to look into the room, the rotten timbers collapsed, plummetting him down ten feet into the room.

As he felt the timbers give away, Tony realized his anger. He kept his hand on his gun to keep from losing it, and as he hit the floor, he rolled against the wall. For an instant he was dazed and blinded by dust and debris. Pushing himself to his knees, he stared into the murky light that came in through the porthole window.

"Hold it right there, Regan!" Veldon's voice grated.

Tony got slowly to his feet. Veldon was standing in the corner near the window, with Ruby held in front of him as a shield. Tony felt a mixture of hate and pity fuse within him. Ruby's red hair was disheveled. Her face was dirtied and bruised from the brutal treatment she had received. At sight of Tony, her brown eyes shone and tears glittered on the lashes. Her dress was torn, exposing her white shoulder, but there was courage and defiance in every line of her body.

"You dared to do do that to her?" Tony said in a deadly voice.

"Just fork over the money, and I'll let her go."

Veldon had his bandaged arm clamped around Ruby's breast, holding her tightly against him. Tony remembered Ruby's warning that Veldon could shoot fast with his left hand.

"Let her go, Veldon, and you walk out of here alive," Tony said. "Take your filthy hands off her."

"She's my woman. Ask anybody. Do you think I never touched her before?"

Ruby said angrily, "He's a liar, Tony. I never was his woman."

"She was my woman until you came messing around," Veldon said. "You can have her for ten thousand dollars."

"Did you kill Pop Smith, Veldon?" Tony said, stalling for time.

"I never saw him. Folger went after him. Give me the ten thousand dollars. It's not yours, anyway; you swindled Carl out of it. When Asp said you didn't have it with you, I figured you had left it with Ruby. But she didn't have it. I turned her place upside down, and it wasn't there."

"So you beat her, you cowardly buzzard."

"I'm not going to argue. I'll give you five seconds to fork over the money; then you both get it."

Tony figured his chances. Veldon was crouched behind Ruby's slim, straight figure so that most of him was covered. Tony tried to tell Ruby to move, to struggle, anything to give him a chance of hitting Veldon. He had to tell her with his eyes to keep Veldon off guard. As though she read his mind, Ruby bowed her head and sank her teeth into Veldon's wrist. Veldon, surprised by her sudden movement, uttered a curse. He raised his gun to fire at the same time. Tony's gun jumped into his hand. His bullet fanned Ruby's red tresses as it barely missed her head and smashed into Veldon's bovine face. Veldon's bullet plowed into the littered floor as he sagged down. He tried to bring his gun back up to kill Ruby, intent on taking her with him in death. Tony shot again, swiftly and with deadly aim.

The bullet shot off part of Veldon's skull.

Ruby tore herself out of Veldon's slackening arm; with a sob of relief and joy, she ran into Tony's arms, clutched him hungrily and sobbed out her gratitude against his chest. He stroked her head, talking to her softly and reassuringly.

"It's over, honey. Thank God it's over." In that moment he knew where his love lay. He was holding it in his arms. And then his lips were on hers.

"He tried to make me give him the money, but I refused. He couldn't find where I had hidden it. He threatened me, slapped me, and when I tried to get away he almost tore my dress off."

"It's all right, honey. You should have given him the money."

"It wouldn't have done any good. He would have killed me then. He insisted no man could have me if I denied him. He kept me alive to use as a pawn."

"How long have you been out here?"

"It was still dark when he came to the shop. I didn't know who it was at the door. I slipped on this dress, and when I opened the door he forced his way in," she said brokenly. "He forced me to come here with him before anybody was stirring in town. He hid the horses in the ruins of the church."

"Come on, darling; we're getting out of here," Tony said, the endearment coming easily to lips still warm from her kisses.

When they reached town, he stopped at Finney's

furniture store and told Finney what had happened. The dark shadow of death still lurked in Tony's eyes.

"I'm not holding a grudge against you, boy," Finney said, cowering under Tony's grim stare. "I lost that money fair and square."

"I'm not worried about you and the money you lost, Finney. Go out to the old mission. You'll find Vern Veldon's body in the next to the last room of the wing. I'll pay for his funeral," Tony said grimly.

"Why? Why should you pay for his funeral?" Ruby asked. "He would have killed you."

"A dead man has no enemies, honey."

At Ruby's place, they went inside to the shambles Veldon had left.

"Get the money, Red, and then I'm taking you out of here until it is all straightened up again."

Ruby smiled. "Where do you think the money is?"

"I'll be doggoned if I know. It looks like every place has been ransacked."

Tony shuddered to think what Ruby had gone through the night before, with Veldon tearing the place to pieces. Because of him Pop Smith was dead. Because of him Ruby had been manhandled. Because of him Wilma would be the victim of Carl Dirkes' wrath. He had to reverse the brutal process somehow. At least for Ruby it was over; he would see to that.

"Veldon couldn't find it because it wasn't in the building."

"You didn't put it in the bank? Carl Dirkes could

grab it easy there."

"Come with me."

She stepped outside and stopped by the rain barrel, which was half full of water that was scummed over. It was the same water Tony had poured on Veldon's head a couple of days before.

"Roll up your sleeve and reach down in there," Ruby ordered.

Tony rolled and reached. He came up with a fruit jar that had been weighted with rocks, and on top of the rocks was the money, folded into a tight wad. The lid of the jar had been screwed on tightly.

"Well, I'll be!" Tony exclaimed. "And you let him ransack the house and beat you when the money was out here?"

"You wouldn't want a woman you couldn't trust, would you, darling?"

"I wouldn't want a woman who would die for a wad of money, either." He grinned.

"It wasn't the money I was fighting for, Tony. It was for you—for us. It was for honor-bright. If Veldon had gotten hold of the money, he would have taken me with him, anyway. He was determined no other man should have me. But until he found the money I was safe, and you were safe."

Tony shook his head. "Put on a whole dress. I'll be right back."

Ruby's reasoning had been sound, he realized that, but he still felt guilty because of the horror she had endured. Somehow he had to subdue the trouble he had resurrected around Sabado. He had not created the trouble; it had been there all along. But it had been concealed, like a festering sore. He had merely opened the sore to let the poison drain out. Tomorrow the Association rep would be there to make the cattle inspection. There was sure to be trouble, and maybe out of that trouble would come the answer.

He went into Lupe's kitchen and found her standing over the steaming stove, preparing the noon menu.

"You run away pronto after *desayuno* thees morning. You gobble the ham and eggs like wan peeg. Deed you find *Señorita* Meeler?"

Tony told Lupe what had happened. Lupe threw up her hands, mixing spoon and all.

"Madre de Dios!" she exclaimed, spraying the kitchen with gravy. "Where she now?"

"She's putting on another dress. I'm taking her out to the Wilsons' with me. Can you get a woman to clean and straighten up her place in the next day or so?"

"I theenk my seester she be happy for job."

"Can we have some lunch to take with us, Lupe?"

"I feex pronto, wan box lonch. You make for picnic?"

"She hasn't eaten since last night. She can eat on the way. I want to get her out of town before Vern Veldon's death becomes known. I told Finney, and he'll spread it around once he gets the body back here," Tony explained. "She'll be safe with Kate Wilson."

When Ruby was dressed, Tony took her key to Lupe so that Lupe's sister could get in through the front door. The back door he nailed shut until the lock could be repaired. Riding beside Ruby, Tony felt elated, but afraid of his elation. He still had one grisly job ahead of him, a job from which he might not emerge alive. Once he got on the open range with the inspection cavvy, the outcome would be in the lap of the gods. Carl Dirkes would be there with Folger. Wilson would be backed by him, Tony and Bengo. There would be the Association representative. Six or seven men on a touchy mission. If Dirkes didn't know of Folger's rustling of Wilson's stock, he might charge a frame-up. Folger, to cover his own dirty work, might start a fight.

When they reached Cherry Creek, the sun was still high, and Tony pulled up his horse. He wanted to savor this hour with Ruby, even though he could not express his love or ask for her acceptance. A man on the eve of his possible execution has no right to burden the living with hopes or promises that could not be kept. To be near her was enough, to see the emotion in her clear brown eyes; to see the expression of her full red lips when she talked; to see the sun shining on the burnished copper of her hair. All this he could accept without obligation on either side.

"Let's eat lunch here by the creek," he suggested, and Ruby readily complied, letting him lift her from the saddle.

As they ate the tasty lunch Lupe had prepared, Tony

told her about his fight with Asp in the water and of Asp's confession about the holdup. They talked about old times, and he noticed the subtle change in her spirits and manner when Wilma came into the conversation.

"Tony," she said pensively, "you can never truly love another woman while Wilma is alive and available."

"Available? What are you talking about? She's about as available as the moon. Dirkes will never give her up alive."

"Will you? You might try to, but will your heart give her up?"

Tony pondered this for a moment. Then he told her in detail about his confrontation with Wilma in the cabin, and how Kent Wilson had seen them and perhaps heard them.

"You say she hopes to get a divorce?" Ruby asked, surprised.

"She'll never get it. She went to Fred Powers to file suit, not knowing that Fred Powers is Dirkes' lawyer in Prescott. Powers will tell Dirkes, and Dirkes will prevent any attempt at divorce. I'm afraid for Wilma. If Kent heard her call me Tony Egan before he saw us embracing, and he told about it, the truth would reach Carl's ears. And what he would do to Wilma I'm afraid to think."

"You say she married Carl to save you from a hangman's noose?"

"That's what she said. I believed her."

"And to think I have ignored and despised her these five years, thinking she had married Dirkes for for his money and position." Tears came to her eyes. "Doesn't—that put you so far in her debt that you could never reject her?"

"It was she who sent me into the ambush at Dirkes' ranch. She feels her sacrifice made up for her mistake in misjudging Dirkes."

"Is that how you feel?"

"What are we talking about, Ruby?" he asked her softly. "Are we talking about Wilma, or are we talking about us?"

"Wilma's ghost stands between us, Tony."

"I'm not so sure about that. People change. I felt a change in Wilma when I confessed my identity in the cabin. Her life with Carl must have had some influence on her."

"But not on you. I know how loyal and honest you are. Her sacrifice would be a yolk about your neck forever."

"Let's be honest and talk straight. The past can never be changed, and to let the future be warped and riddled by things that might have been but never existed is a waste of precious time. Suppose everything were settled; suppose Wilma suddenly decided she was content with her lot; suppose Dirkes had no reason or desire to kill me; supposing all that—what would your answer be if I told you that I love *you?*"

She looked at him, her heart in her moist eyes. "Suppose we wait until there are no supposes. Then ask me, Tony."

They finished lunch and rode the rest of the way home in a pensive mood.

CHAPTER TWELVE

Mrs. Wilson greeted them in the front hall of the big house and welcomed them warmly. Tony explained what had happened in as few words as possible, and when he was through, Kate Wilson threw up her hands.

"For land's sake!" she exclaimed, "what things go on! You poor girl, you must be spent and hungry."

"We ate on the way out, Kate. We can wait until supper. Where's Bud, your husband?"

"He went into town to meet the afternoon stage from Prescott and bring the Cattlemen's rep out here for the count in the morning. There's more been going on than you realize. Come into the parlor."

They followed Kate into the parlor and stood there for a moment, mute and bewildered. Wilma Dirkes was seated on the sofa, her face white and concerned. Kent Wilson, his young body stiff and defensive, stood by the stone fireplace. Tony saw the look that passed between Ruby and Wilma.

"What are you doing here, Wilma?" Tony asked.

"Carl heard about you and me in the cabin, Tony.

He knows who you are. He's sworn to kill you or me or maybe both of us. The cook warned me, and I came over here before Carl could find me."

Kent, his young face twisted with remorse, said, "I didn't tell Dirkes about you, honest I didn't. I mentioned it in the bunkhouse as a kind of joke. I didn't think Dirkes would hear of it."

"He was bound to hear about it sooner or later, Kent." Tony shrugged.

"If you go on that cattle count tomorrow, Dirkes will kill you," Wilma said. "He'll blame me, too, because I talked him out of hanging you after that phony trial.

"Killing is a two-way thing, Wilma. I killed Vern Veldon this morning."

"You what?"

"It was to save me," Ruby said. "Veldon kidnapped me and held me hostage in the old mission, trying to force Tony to turn over ten thousand dollars to him."

Tony went on to explain just what had happened, beginning with the ransacking of Ruby's shop.

"The thing grows worse and worse. Veldon was one of Carl's right-hand men. His death will give Carl one more reason to kill you, Tony," Wilma said. She added in a pleading voice, "Why don't you go away, Tony? Let things work themselves out. You can come back later, when the time is right."

"The time is always right, Wilma; it's the men in the time who are wrong. If I traipsed out now, with Carl knowing what he does, he'd send a man to hunt me down and kill me like a coyote in a burrow. I won't be alone on the cattle count; Wilson will be there with Bengo. I'm a special agent with the stage company; I've got a badge which gives me some authority. The Association rep is a deputy of the United States marshal. I'm arresting Dirkes and Folger tomorrow for robbery and murder. I've got all the evidence I need on the stage holdups, and Folger killed Pop Smith after the old man left town yesterday."

"Oh, no!" Kate exclaimed. "That poor old man."

"I feel a little responsible for that," Tony said. "I rigged the deal."

"What are you trying to do, Tony—play God?" Wilma asked. "You're taking the blame for others' transgressions; you're out to scourge the crooks from the temple; you're out to collect everybody's sins and put them neatly in your own soul. Don't feel sorry for me; don't blame yourself because Folger is a killer."

"I suppose I should have let Veldon have his way with Ruby?"

"At least she can reward you; nobody else will."

"I'm going upstairs to see Abe Jones," Tony said. "He may want to ride on the cattle count tomorrow."

"He's locked in," Kent said. "The key is in the door."

"Where's Lucy?"

"In her room, I suppose."

Tony went upstairs to the back bedroom and unlocked the door. He entered the room to find it empty. The window in the back wall was open. Tony went to the window and looked out. The window opened on the lean-to kitchen at the back of the house, and beside the window, on the kitchen roof, with his back against the wall of the house, sat Abe. The low-hanging sun glistened off his kinky head as he industriously cleaned his rifle.

"What are you doing there, Abe?"

"Takin' what sun I can git. They got me locked up lak' a stray bull. Figgered I'd clean mah guns case yo 'all got sense enough to take me along on the cattle inspection."

"Rest here one more night, Abe, and we'll see about it."

Abe was thumbing shells into the magazine of his Winchester and levering them out again.

"I got this gun of mine workin' smooth as oil," Abe said smugly.

"If I let you come on the cattle count, you've got to promise not to start a ruckus. Folger's the man who shot you, and he'll be there. If there's going to be trouble, let them start it."

"Amen, brother."

"I'm going down to the bunkhouse to talk to Bengo."

"Ah cain't see too good from here, pardner," Abe said, "on account of the trees, but somethin's goin' on down theah. They's been some comin's and goin's. Looked like Baudry and Fats was ridin' out with theah bedrolls. You be careful if you go down theah, heah?"

"There'll be no trouble here, Abe. If Dirkes means to make trouble, he'll wait until we find the doctored brands, and that will give him an excuse."

Tony avoided the parlor and headed for the stairs that went down outside in back of the house. He wondered what the women were doing. Had Ruby told Wilma that she knew at last why Wilma had married Dirkes? Had Wilma forgiven Ruby for her rejection of her? His ears should have been burning; they were probably picking him to pieces by now. Remembering Abe's warning, he pulled his gun around and slid it from the holster a couple of times to make sure it worked smoothly.

With an uneasy feeling, he walked across the yard toward the bunkhouse and the barn. He saw no one stirring, but he gave it no thought. The men could be in the bunkhouse getting ready for supper. Then he remembered Aby saying that Baudry and Fats had ridden out with their blanket rolls. Why? Why should they leave so suddenly they had not even stayed for supper? He passed the last of the cottonwood trees and entered the wider area between the bunkhouse and the barn. Suddenly he felt vulnerable and naked, with nothing to hide behind. He chided himself for his fears and moved ahead. He reached a spot between the bunkhouse and the barn when the devil showed his ugly face.

Carl Dirkes came from the dark entrance to the barn, his face a mask of rock-hard fury, his movements deliberate. Folger's lean figure appeared at the corner of the bunkhouse. From behind the water trough near the corral rose the figure of Asp, whom he had beaten and

almost drowned. For one clear second the picture was
stamped indelibly on his brain. It was the ambush all
over again, it was a replay of that grim, deadly moment
five years before. This time the results would be final.
Dirkes spoke, and his voice cut like a knife across the
yard.

"You've deviled me for the last time, Tony Egan.
I should have killed you the last time, but I listened
to the voice of a girl—your girl! Now you've come
to take her away from me, to jail me and cut me down
to nothing. There's only one thing wrong with it: you're
too late!"

Tony saw the three men in front of him, each of them
with a reason to kill him. He could never kill them
all. One—maybe two, but three was a stacked deck
against him. He watched Dirkes' hand. Carl must have
given orders that nobody shoot until he had the first try.
Carl wanted to kill Tony himself, venting his hate and
anger in the letting of blood. Carl's feet braced, and
Tony saw his shoulder twitch. Then Tony made his draw.

As he drew and fired, Tony threw himself aside,
landing on his knees. Carl hesitated like a man struck
with a rock in the middle of his guts. Carl's bullet cut
a swath in Tony's left shoulder. He heard Folger firing
before the sound of Carl's gun had died. He twisted and
fired at Folger and saw Folger fall to one knee. He
couldn't see Asp. Carl was lying on the ground, brac-
ing his gun across arm. Tony, back on his feet, and
weaving as he walked forward, sent another bullet

into Carl's prone body. The big body relaxed, the hate and fury drained from it.

Another slug hit Tony and knocked him back on his buttocks. He saw Folger crawling toward him, and he fired a desperate shot that hit Folger on the top of his black head. Folger lay face down on the dirt. Tony tried to focus his eyes on Asp, but the yard was spinning about him. He tried to shake the haze from his eyes. Asp was close to him, looking down. Tony lifted the muzzle of his gun and fired. He didn't hear the shot. He heard only the echo of the shot from far off. Asp was lifted off his feet and thrown violently to the ground, a mound of flesh that quivered and lay still.

Tony felt himself dropping into a deep hole, a bottomless pit sans pain, sans blood, sans sight and sans dreams. His last vision was of Abe Jones on the roof of the kitchen with a smoking rifle in his hands.

When Tony came to, he was in the parlor, and the lamps had already been lit. He was lying on the sofa. He looked up into the cone of light above him and called a name.

"Ruby—Ruby darling."

"I'm here, Tony."

Her radiant face swam into view before his eyes, but he couldn't lift his arms to draw her to him. He turned his head. Wilma was bathing a wound in his side.

"Why don't you kiss him, Ruby?" Wilma said in a not unkindly voice.

Ruby kissed him, and he savored the kiss even as he felt Wilma's smooth fingers gently touch his arm. He lay still a moment until Wilma, with Ruby's help, had his wound bandaged.

"How did the fight end?" he asked.

"You killed Carl, Tony," Wilma said, and there was no accusation in her voice.

So he had killed Carl Dirkes as he had been destined to do. That killing erected a final barrier between him and Wilma. The realization of this brought him no despair. All he could see was Ruby's red head, Ruby's brown eyes. He was happy to see the two women friends once more. Wilma drew back and surveyed him, and he saw the change in her, the pride and assurance of a woman who had suddenly come into power and knew it.

"You killed Folger, too. He had Pop Smith's money on him."

"But Asp had me dead in his sights, and my gun was empty."

From behind the girls came Abe's voice. "Reckon if I hadn't been on the kitchen roof with my rifle, he would have plugged you, pahdner."

"Thanks, Abe; I won't forget it." Then his tone changed. "That ten thousand dollars I have that was part of the money I swindled from Carl—I want you to have it back, Wilma. You're boss of the Box-X now."

"I mean to run it honestly, too. I'm giving you back the land and water Dirkes stole from you. You can keep the ten thousand dollars. Carl owed you that much for the years you have lost."

"Crooked money is no way to start a dream," Tony objected.

"Take it as a loan, then. Pay me back when you can, when you and Ruby have your ranch going good."

Ruby, looking at Tony with adoration, said, "I'll keep the dress shop going until we get built up, honey."

"I'll keep my special agent's job on the stage for a time, too."

"You'll take the money, and you'll build the house you should have had by now. You'll clear ground, and you'll build a fence. I'm giving you back the cattle Dirkes stole from you and the normal increase they would have had."

"Why are you doing all this, Wilma?" Ruby asked.

Wilma smiled. "What are neighbors for if not to be neighborly?"

"How can we repay you?" Tony said.

"You can sing in the Sabada Queen now and then."

"But Pop Smith's money, you've got to take that back."

"I'm going to build a church and a school with it. What was Pop's first name, Tony?"

"Reckon I never heard it. Everybody called him Pop."

"All right; we'll call it the 'Pop Smith Public School,'" Wilma said.